the song of arthur

Robert Leeson is a versatile and acclaimed children's author whose works range from Grange Hill novels to science fiction, fantasy and retellings of traditional stories, such as his *Smart Girls*, shortlisted for the Guardian Children's Fiction Award 1994. In 1985 he received the prestigious Eleanor Farjeon Award for Services to Children's Literature.

Books by the same author

The Story of Robin Hood
All the Gold in the World
Silver's Revenge
Red, White and Blue

For younger readers

The Amazing Adventures of Idle Jack
Lucky Lad
Smart Girls
Smart Girls Forever
Why's the Cow on the Roof?

the song of
arthur

ROBERT LEESON

WALKER BOOKS
AND SUBSIDIARIES

LONDON • BOSTON • SYDNEY

For Frederick and Christine

Historic places on this map are shown in roman
lettering; legendary or mythical places (where their
location can be guessed at) are shown in *italics*.
But many places named in this story belong in the
Otherworld, which, in Arthur's time, was
both everywhere and nowhere.

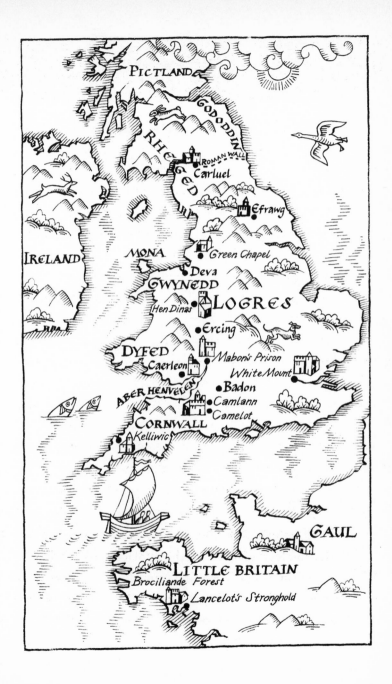

contents

camelot in its glory

the questing spirit revived

the last battle

prologue

There is no quiet like the stillness after battle.

Silently we carried Arthur our chieftain to the dark shore and laid him down where the sand was soft as velvet.

Old Bedwyr unhooked the great sword from Arthur's waist and carried it off to give back to she from whom it came.

I cleaned the blood from Arthur's wounds and counted them, fifteen in all, honourable wounds. His face was pale as always, save when he was angry. Well, he would rage no more.

As I took off my cloak and placed it under his head, he opened one eye and whispered.

"Little Tal. Not a scratch on you. She guards you well."

"As she'll tend you," I whispered.

"Don't weep. Sing to me." His eyes closed.

I sang to him softly, as I sang to Merlin long ago in the forest, of battles, adventures and love unending.

While I sang, I heard the whisper of ripples on the sand and knew the Dark Queens were coming.

The boat, its prow like a black swan, drew into land.

They sat silent and veiled, most potent Three of the Otherworld, three who had shaped my life, inspiring, protecting, befriending.

Slowly we lifted our prince and laid him down among them.

Slowly the craft drew away from the shore to vanish into the night.

At the last moment, without knowing what I did, I moved to climb on board, but one of the Three raised her hand.

"No, Little One. Not you. Not yet. Go sing your Song of Arthur."

part one

in search of arthur

how I took up my sword and my harp

When I was a boy, the great kingdoms of the North went to war. The land they fought over was not even enough to bury the dead. For days the ravens made the air horrid with their croaking.

In the fighting, my father and his lord died and when all was over I searched for his body among the fallen. By the time I found him all his armour, armlets and the gold torque round his neck had been stripped from his body. But his sword I found in a cleft in the rocks where he had hidden it before he died. The blade was so long it reached to my shoulder, so I slung it on my back. His harp I already carried, for he had given it to me before the battle as if he had known it would be his last.

When the fallen were buried I went to the dead lord's hall to pledge my loyalty to his widow. I found her by the outer gate, surrounded by her servants, all women or men who were either too old or badly wounded. Horses and mule carts loaded with food and clothes stood by.

When I dropped on one knee, her kind eye fell on the sword and the harp that hung at my back. She put a hand on my head.

"If you come with us, Little One, you must leave that great sword behind."

I stared at her without understanding. She pointed to a baby who lay asleep in a servant's arms.

"Peredur is all I have. His father and six brothers are all gone. He shall grow up knowing nothing of war."

"But lady, who will protect you?"

She looked down at the sword on my back and smiled again.

"We shall travel far away to where there are no men of war. There we shall begin our life again, tending the fields and dying in our beds."

Placing her hand on my head again as if to bless me, she said, "If it is battle and songs of battle you seek, you must look for them elsewhere."

With these words she mounted her horse, gave the signal to her people and, while I watched, they vanished into the wilderness. I never saw my lady again – but little Peredur – that's another story.

go find the boar of cornwall!

In my homeland, death waited. So I turned to the south. The great forest took me in.

Hungry, weary, torn by thorns, foul from the marshes I stumbled into, I lay down to sleep when I could go no further. Above me the great trees cut off the sun. I knew neither day nor night but wandered on.

Waking in grey half-light, I saw a wolf, fangs bared, yellow eyes glaring. In terror I leapt up, clutching my sword. But the wolf turned and trotted into the forest gloom and I followed mile after mile. When I sank down from weariness, the wolf stopped and lay down not far away. At last we came into a grassy glade, where an apple-tree grew, its fruit glowing, though it was midwinter. Beneath its branches sat a man. I knew him, a warrior, fierce and brave. But now ragged, dirty, hair before his eyes.

"Lailoken!" I called. "Why are you here?"

He rose and glared madly at me. "Lailoken is dead. All are dead. I no longer care if the sky falls and the sea rushes up to meet it."

The wolf sat at his feet and he stroked its grey head.

14

"I am a wolf and live among wolves."

Then he stroked the apple-tree bark.

"The tree hides me. They will not find me. Now brother kills brother and the Red Dragon tears itself to pieces."

"Lailoken," I began but he seized me by my shoulder.

"That is not my name. No one knows my name till the time is ripe."

His grip grew softer, his voice quieter.

"Alas, the Red Dragon is near its death. The White Dragon from across the sea will destroy it. Rivers will run blood, trees grow in cornfields, wolves roam in cities. Listen! Buried kings will be dug from their graves. The Island will be drenched in tears."

For a moment he was silent. Then he raised his arms.

"But the Boar of Cornwall will trample the White Dragon. You shall sing the Boar's praises, Little One. Go find him."

"Where shall I find him?"

He seemed not to hear me.

"Get up into that oak-tree, boy. Cut off and throw down the highest branch."

I did not understand, but did as he told me. Climbing the tree, I used my father's sword to cut the branch and threw it down. The madman whose name was not Lailoken caught it. I called down.

"Tell me where to find..."

"You shall see," he called back and then vanished from my sight.

voyaging across the water

I looked out from the tops of the oak-tree and saw beyond the forest a broad river shining in the sun. On the water rode a ship. Sailors were busy loading her and trimming the sails. I knew what Lailoken meant I should see.

I forgot my hunger and my weariness. Climbing from the tree, I ran, stumbled on roots and blundered through briars till in an hour I reached the shore. The ship was bound for Dyfed. I went on board and soon she sailed out into the open sea.

There were others too. Six monks in grey robes, plump jolly lads not much older than me. They prayed morning, noon and night and at times they howled like dogs – or so it seemed to my ears. Often they ate – and well. Still, they shared their food with me for they saw I was starving. They eyed my harp. Would I go with them? I shook my head and told them of my search for the Boar of Cornwall.

"The Red Ravager," said one. The others frowned – told him to be quiet. Someone laughed. A girl leaned on the side of the ship, bright-eyed, hair like bronze, dressed in blue. I spoke to her, but she skipped away, now on one foot then on the other, as the ship rolled on the waves.

At first a strong breeze bore us to the south. A day and a night we sailed under a clear sky. But on the next day the heavens grew dark as night, the wind began to shriek like a wounded beast, the sea flung itself over the ship side and we on board were thrown about like toys.

The monks fell to their knees and prayed to their Maker. The sailors called on Manawydan the sea god to save them. I clung to the mast. In that moment when the sea and sky changed places I saw the girl. She was dancing, yes dancing, in the prow. It seemed to me that nothing could save her from drowning.

I let go my hold on the mast and leapt towards her. She only laughed as if it were a game. The ship kicked up its heels like a war-horse and I was hurled into the sea.

I cried out in terror as the waves swallowed me, though I knew my cries were useless. My Northern gods were far away and could not hear me. But a strange thing happened. My body rose to the surface and I seemed to see the smiling face of the girl from the ship.

I lay on my back, arms folded across my chest like the sea-otter. The sea raised me up and swept me on. Like the sea-otter, I slept and when I woke I lay on rocks with the water draining from me. How it came about I do not know but I was alive.

Before me the land stretched out. Valleys and moors

cloaked in fog. Climbing up, I saw far away on a hilltop a great fortress, its ramparts wreathed in mist, its top catching the morning sun.

arthur, the boar

Setting my face towards the hill, I marched, clothes clinging chill to my limbs. Now it seemed nearer and clearer. Now, as I dropped into the gullies, it vanished altogether. Sheep bleated nearby and I came across a boy tending them. I pointed.

"What is that stronghold?"

He eyed me quickly then turned away.

"You must be a stranger. That's Kelliwic, the lair of the Boar of Cornwall."

Leaving him, I hurried on. Yet the fortress came no nearer. Mist swirled. Woods and marshes surrounded me. I lost my way and wandered wildly.

I heard dogs bark, then men shouting, horses neighing. Close by, there came a fearful crashing and painful grunting.

Breaking through bushes, I came out into a clearing by a marshy lake. Now a breeze blew the mist into shreds.

Closer came the sound of snarling and branches

snapping. Out into the open rushed a great hart, tawny hide smeared with mud, muzzle stained with blood. Behind it bayed the hounds, nearer, nearer.

The beast halted, uncertain. Then as the sound of dogs grew louder, it turned and plunged into the lake. A moment later a great hound appeared, larger than a pony, its jaws dripping foam. As it turned towards the water, some madness made me unsling my harp and strike two notes high and clear.

The great dog turned from his quarry and leapt towards me, growling horribly. I fled to a tree nearby and sprang in its branches like a squirrel, while the savage jaws snapped beneath me. Barking madly, the hound-pack burst into the open. Behind them came four figures on horseback. I held my breath.

Three were men in bright chequered cloth, gold armlets glinting. The first rider was huge, thick hair bristling on his arms, his face broad and pale. Next to him, a tall fair-haired handsome warrior with a fierce, cruel face. The third was one-armed. Carrying a hunting spear, he held his reins in his teeth. But the fourth rider was a woman, her hair flame-red like her dress. I stared, for the face was that of the girl on the ship. Yet older, like sister or mother.

The giant rider laughed.

"The hart is up the tree."

He looked up at me. I have never seen eyes so sharp, so commanding.

"Come down, lad. Come. Cabal will not eat you – unless I say he may."

The three laughed. The woman only smiled.

As I dropped to the ground, the fair-haired man said:

"A minstrel!"

The third man spat out his reins.

"Yes, and a warrior. Look at the sword."

Their laughter made me red with shame. The giant's look and voice were not unkind.

"Where are you from?"

"From Efrawg, lord."

"What are you doing here?" The tone was sharp.

"My father and his lord fell in battle."

"Very well. Come to my hall at Kelliwic tonight. You shall tell the story."

All four turned their horses. Followed by the hounds, they vanished in the mist, the leader shouting:

"Tell them Arthur sent you."

arthur's hall

I followed the sound of their laughter, the jingle of the horses, until it died away and I was alone in the forest and the mist. Trudging on, I kept up my spirits with a song I made in my head, and thought I would sing it in Arthur's hall at Kelliwic.

My lady of Efrawg had sent me away. The wolf led me to Lailoken. Lailoken told me of the White Dragon from over the sea who would oppress the Red Dragon, until the Boar of Cornwall trampled it under his feet. *Go find him*, he told me. Lailoken had shown me the ship. The girl with red-gold hair had lured me into the sea. And the sea had carried me to the feet of Arthur.

I sang the words in my head many times as I struggled on through the forest. But at last I was free of the bushes and briars and came into the open. Before me a great green hill reared up. Rampart after rampart, great walls of earth and rock ringed it round, rising to the summit where the stronghold, massive in timber and stone, towered against the setting sun.

On all sides from the fields round about streamed people. Young and old, some driving sheep and pigs, some mules with great loads, pushed their way in through the first gateway. Beyond was a broad ditch. The track spiralled round the hill, climbing upwards to another gate. Here were sentries who nodded all comers through. They did not even notice me. Once more I climbed round the great circle of the ditch and to a third gate. Here I was seen. One guard reached out and tapped my harp.

"A minstrel!"

The others laughed. I bent my head and climbed round and upwards to the last gateway. Inside the ramparts was a wide space of open ground, crowded and noisy; houses, granaries, fires, children playing. And over all towered the hall, its doorpost timbers tall as ships' masts, carved and decorated in rich colours.

Huge doors stood open. The sun's rays and the smoking flare of torches showed a wide floor strewn with green rushes, long tables and at the centre a great fire of pine logs and a long couch covered in white sheepskin. Men and women hurried to and fro carrying platters heaped with meat, savoury and steaming. The smell made my empty stomach groan.

Eagerly I stepped forward. But in that moment I was stopped in my tracks. The butt of a spear sprang like magic across my chest and a deep voice said, "Not a step further, little man."

Barring my way was a man little taller than me but as broad as two men. His eyes glared, but I could tell he was not angry and so I spoke boldly. "Lord Arthur wanted me to sing. I am a minstrel from the North."

His laughter crashed like a wave on the shore. Then he rubbed his eyes and reached out to touch the sword-hilt at my shoulder. "A warrior too," he said.

"That was my father's," I said.

His hand drew back and rested on my arm. He understood me.

"They call me Mightygrasp. I am doorkeeper. No one enters here before Arthur. You can wait here until he calls you. Are you hungry?"

I nodded. He shouted to the servants and they brought me bread and meat. As I ate, the darkness folded down outside, and inside the warmth and light of the hall grew. Then came voices, laughter, and the doorkeeper nudged me.

"Here he comes."

Into the torch glare strode Arthur, now splendid in a tunic of blue, red-gold at his throat and arms, hair and beard combed. A crowd followed on.

I heard the doorkeeper whisper, "He with the yellow hair. That's Kai, cold and stubborn, worth a hundred in a fight. Never wearies. The one-armed – that's Bedwyr. If he had two arms, he'd be an army on his own."

"And the lady?" I asked, my eyes fixed on her face as she strode past.

"That is Morgaine, Arthur's kin, so they say. She goes like the wind through flame. Beware of her."

Now three boys, my age, came past, shoving their

23

way through the guests, fighting with each other.

One, slender, fair and handsome, flung himself into the place at Arthur's side.

"That's Amr. Arthur's heir. Watch out for him."

The second, lean and pale.

"That's Gwydre. Sits a horse as if born in the saddle."

And the third, stocky, quiet, dark.

"Llachau – braver and better than his father knows."

"All his sons?" I asked.

The doorkeeper chuckled.

"Three sons, three mothers."

As we talked, the hall filled, plates clattered, the horns with mead were carried round and the chatter from the tables grew to a clamour as each one strove to be heard. Quite suddenly there was silence.

A woman's voice called, "A story, a tale."

There was a roar of approval. A white-haired man rose at a table close to Arthur's couch. I saw he held a harp. But Arthur waved him down. "No, no. I'll hear the boy from Efrawg."

"But the oldest sings first," the white-beard protested.

"Not tonight. I'll hear the nightingale from the North."

The doorkeeper tapped me on the shoulder. But I was gripped by fear. The words flew from my head like moths. My lips were sealed with stupidity. The silence nailed me to the ground.

"Where is he hiding?" Arthur grew impatient.

So did the doorkeeper. With a mighty shove he sent

me flying into the space before the couch, to fall flat on my face. Arthur's boys began to chuckle but the father hushed them. "Sing, lad," he said, kindly but sternly.

How can I describe what came next? As I scrambled to my feet and dragged the harp from my back, I saw again my father lying on the ground, arms and legs covered with blood. My eyes, my head, my body filled with tears.

Blinded, I struck false notes. My voice broke as I opened my mouth, giving wild, ugly sounds that made no sense. I stopped in an awful silence.

The white-haired man said quietly, "I hear no nightingale. Seagull maybe or a crow, but no nightingale."

Laughter from all sides followed me as I ran away half-dead with shame into the darkness.

morgaine's magic

That night I lay under the winter stars and would have frozen if someone had not thrown an old cloak over me. Sleep came only when I made up my mind to steal away from Kelliwic at first light. I could not bear to see another day in Arthur's stronghold.

It was not to be, for in the grey dawn I was awakened with a kick. Three faces looked down on me. Amr's handsome and haughty, Gwydre's carefree and mocking. Llachau's eyes were friendly, but he stood apart from the others. Amr spoke like a prince who knows his power. I remembered what Mightygrasp, the doorkeeper, had said about Arthur and his sons. The father had an eagle's eye but did not see those things close by.

"Get up!" ordered Amr. "Let us see if you are as skilled with that sword as with the harp." Gwydre laughed. Llachau did not.

"Give me room," I said. I spoke as boldly as I could. I knew and so did Amr with his cold blue eyes that I did not dare draw my father's sword. I could only take flight. But how? They stood between me and the gate. Step by step I drew back and step by step Amr and Gwydre followed me. Amr had a hand on his sword-hilt, as if taunting me. All at once they halted. I moved three more paces till my back struck timber. But they moved no closer.

Behind me rose a house of lofty oak pillars, like a temple. A narrow door opened to my left. My eyes could not believe what they saw. In the dark opening stood the girl from the ship. She smiled. Was I dreaming? But she said, "Come," and beckoned. Forgetting my tormentors I followed her inside and the oak door thundered shut behind me.

"Come," she said again. Taking my hand, she led me

26

through a maze of narrow passages. They turned like a snake now left, now right. Around me all was dark as night. She drew me on and blindly I followed. We came to a high-ceilinged chamber, light as day, though I could see no windows. Round its walls were shelves with strange jars and fluids glittering green and purple. Right at the centre stood a cauldron of dark liquid that bubbled, though there was no fire. Letting go my hand, the girl gave me a wooden ladle.

"This may be tended only by a boy who has lost both mother and father. No woman must touch it. Stir and do not spill."

She left me and I stirred as in a dream. Time passed, the chamber darkened, grew light, then dark. I stirred and stirred and then I dozed. A great hissing woke me. The cauldron boiled over. My hand stung as three burning drops flew out. I thrust my fingers to my mouth to cool them.

Light blazed. Shutters fell from the walls like thunder. I saw out over wondrous forests to a shining sea. With a great caw a monstrous crow flew into the chamber, changing as it landed into a dreadful old crone whose black-nailed fingers reached for me.

"Thief!" she shrieked. "You drank my potion. Now I'll eat you."

I was not afraid. Power beyond measure was in me. I changed into a bird and flew out into the sky. She followed as a hawk, I flew down, became a hare, then she a hound. When her breath burned on my neck, I dived into water as a fish, she, an otter, close behind. Back into bird's shape I fell into the chamber once again. I heard her wings beat close. Now I was a grain of wheat so small. I rolled into a dark corner. She screeched.

"There are nine ways I can appear. You shall not escape."

In hen's shape she pecked and pecked until she had me in her beak. I vanished into dark night. Then all was day again. I stood in the high chamber. Morgaine was before me, eyes mocking.

"I have won, Little One. But so have you."

I trembled. She smiled and laid a finger on my forehead.

"You shall have three gifts.

"First, you shall sing like no minstrel before or after you.

"Second, you shall know what other men do not, but you shall not make use of what you know.

"Third, no one shall hurt you if I guard you."

Saying this, she left me suddenly.

I turned to make my way into the maze, but the girl stood there smiling.

"Stay awhile. I am Arian." She touched my shoulder. "Tonight you shall turn the tables on your tormentors."

"How?" I asked, wondering.

"Sit down with me and I will tell you."

how I became arthur's minstrel

That evening, dressed in a tunic of black and gold that Arian had given me, I strode into Arthur's crowded hall, where the flames danced on pine logs and the Boar sat at ease on his fleece-covered couch.

At first no one knew me, but then yellow-haired Kai shouted with laughter:

"The nightingale of the North."

The others roared and began to pelt me with bread crusts. But I laughed back at them. I spoke only to Arthur.

"Lord. I challenge your bards to a contest. Let them sing first. I'll sing after."

How they laughed. None more loudly than Arthur's minstrels. But one-armed Bedwyr spoke up.

"I say. Why not? Good sport, say I."

Arthur was silent for a moment, then he laughed too. "Very well. Let Morvyn begin."

The white-haired bard – he who had called me crow and seagull yesterday – rose and played. But as he sang I fixed my eyes on him. All that came out of his open mouth were stupid "Blrm" noises such as children make.

Try as he might, he could not sing. Red-faced and raging, he sat down. The others followed one by one. And none of them could sing a note. I silenced them one and all.

Arthur looked at me in puzzlement. Amr's blue eyes were round. Arthur spoke.

"Who are you? What are you?"

I struck my harp a true ringing note and I sang:

"I am a salmon in the stream
A coracle on the waves
A blade in the air
A song in the heart
Grain in the crop of a hen
A stag, a snake
Light for the blind
Food for the poor."

When the cheers died down I sang boastfully:

"I know why the earth is green
Why hills echo
Why silver shines.
I know where the cuckoo flies
Why berries are red
What makes smoke rise
What created evil and good."

After I had finished, Arthur said again, "What is your name?"

But Morgaine cried, "Let us name him – Taliesin – Bright Brow."

Arthur turned to his bards.

"Move up, make room for him," he said.

part two

a time of great quests

treasures of
the island

Arthur's gifts fell on me like rain, gold armlets, tunics of rich chequered cloth, the best of food from his table and a roan pony from his winter pasture, which I called Red Runner. Gwydre taught me to break and ride her and when I fell, laughed and lifted me to her. Llachau taught me to use my father's sword, first two-handed, then one-handed as my strength grew.

Amr taught me to keep my wits about me. He did not care for me nor I for him. He had his place next to Arthur as his heir. I had my place next to him by Arthur's favour – as long as that lasted, as long as my songs pleased. But I did not think of tomorrow. I had all that I could wish for. And there was Arian to talk to, in her room in the tall timber maze house, where only I was allowed to enter.

As we sat together on sunlit afternoons she taught me tales and songs the like of which I never heard. When I sang them in the evenings, I gloried in the shouts of praise from the crowded hall. I gloried in the furious, envious glances of the old bards. But most of all I kept my eye on Morgaine sitting among the revellers. Only the tiniest movement of her eyebrow told me I had done well.

I sang of heroes from the far past, of Bran, god-king of the Island of the Mighty, whose deeds outreached all human strength. I praised leaders of our time, Rhydderch Hael, whose sword flamed from hilt to tip, and Arthur's own father, Uther the Pendragon, who had led warbands from west and north and the farthest reach of Logres to the east. Yet I knew one day my greatest song would be of Arthur. He was like no one else, more bear, more boar, than man; reckless yet shrewd, impulsive yet never wild. His star was the brightest in our heaven.

Men followed him because he was ready for any deed. They came from far and near, rich men's sons with their golden armour, hoping for fame, poor men's sons with only their courage, hoping for gifts. None went empty-handed. Arthur raided and defended, not for land but renown. His ships headed for glory or death, men sailed in his wake.

His war-band counted three hundred warriors. But often Kelliwic swarmed with twice that number, eating, drinking, fighting. Kai, keeping order, would have sent the strangers packing, but Arthur said:

"When men no longer come here our name will be forgotten."

Victories bring wealth. Defeat keeps foes quiet.

Peace brought plenty to the fields but idleness and discontent to the fighter.

The more he stayed at home, the more restless Arthur grew. He looked to me for fresh stories, new songs to spur him on to fresh glory. My store began to fail. The white-haired bards looked on with malice, waiting for my fall.

But one day Arian whispered in my ear and that night I sang of the Thirteen Treasures of the Island of the Mighty. My hero's eyes grew huge with wonder.

I sang the Cloak of Invisibility, the Chariot that ran without horses, the Halter to bring any steed to your side, and yet more. The jewelled Salver that would serve only the brave, Bran's Horn with drink everlasting, the Cauldron of Renewal, that brought the dead to life. Last, and I saw the light in Arthur's eyes – the Sword of the Enchanter. These treasures, so I sang, had gone from the Island with the ancient heroes. Now they lay in Annwn, the Otherworld, where no rain fell, nor storm, where the brave never died but feasted day and night.

In the silence at the end of my song, it came into my head to shout:

"Only the greatest heroes can restore them."

A great thunder of cheering broke out. Arthur spoke.

"We will go!"

The oldest bard looked at me with eyes of reproach.

"You have done a terrible thing," he whispered. "The Treasures are beneath the sea. To seek them means death."

But Morgaine, whose ears heard all, called out:

"No – let those who dare go forth."

the quest for
the treasures

Three ships sailed on that fateful voyage, Arthur's own, Prydwen, and two consorts. Three hundred were on board. Five and seventy warriors with gold torques, each with three spearmen. I sailed along with them for the sake of my songs. Those I would sing when we returned laden with the plunder of the Otherworld.

Arthur's three sons were left behind – Amr, his heir, he would not take on such a venture; Amr said if he could not go, neither should Gwydre and Llachau.

We sailed at dawn when the mist lay thick on the sea. We sailed in silence, the waves slid like oil beneath our keels. We sailed where the wind carried us, in blind hope. No one knows where Annwn lies unless the Lords of Annwn choose to reveal it.

We sailed three days and three nights and with each hour that passed, high spirits ebbed away. Some would have turned back, but Arthur would not – and the wind would not let us go. Then on the fourth day with the light, the mist was blown away. The high blue sky thundered till our heads rang. Trumpets sounded. There beyond our prow, appearing out of the green depths, we saw a marvel.

A great glass fortress towered, rampart upon rampart, each crowded with armed men, no less than six thousand rank on rank. Our herald challenged them. Three times his call echoed over the sea as still as the glass tower. But no one answered. Silent they watched.

"Let's attack!" Kai's voice broke the stillness. "There's twenty of them for each of us."

But our laughter rose on high, and Arthur gave the signal. Oars cut the water and our flotilla surged towards the shore and the silent stronghold. But as we reached the shallows the rocks before us split asunder. All three ships were plunged into a mighty cavern, black as night.

Our hearts failed us.

But Arthur cried, "Row!"

Blindly we rowed. The darkness deepened till we could not see our comrades' faces. Behind our sterns the rocks groaned as the cavern mouth closed on us. There was no way back.

"Row!" cried Arthur. Blindly we rowed.

A terrible scream split the air. Chains clattered in the darkness. Our hearts failed us.

"Row!" cried Arthur.

Sunshine flashed into our eyes. Warm air breathed on our faces. Right before us lay an island low and green in the water. Apple-trees glowed, cattle lowed in the meadows. Our keels grounded on gentle golden sands. Gratefully we stood on firm ground, stretching limbs, loosening swords in sheaths. Arthur commanded the spearmen to wait by the ships. The sixty warriors he led forward over the springing turf.

the treasures won and lost

About us birds sang, fountains played. I swear they smelt of mead and wine, not water. In front we saw a splendid hall, four-cornered, of many-coloured wood and stone. Its doors, glowing with precious stones, swung open on a lofty chamber.

Two laden tables each with fourscore places stretched across the room. One was already full with nobly dressed men, all in the prime of life. Yet as I looked I knew that these were all heroes vanished from the earth a thousand years ago.

They bid us sit down and take our ease. As we did, nine maidens, slender and veiled, entered. They bore a jewelled salver with rich food, a carved horn with wine. These passed around, we ate and drank and yet they never emptied. Next came a cauldron, indigo blue with pearls round its rim. The maidens breathed on it and, without fire, it boiled, sending off a sweet aroma. Lastly, two fair-haired youths marched in, holding aloft a sword whose blade sent shafts of lightning crackling through the air.

We marvelled. We ate. We drank. We sang. But in the midst of our carousal our hearts were chilled by a piercing scream and clanking chains that seemed to sound beneath our table.

"Who cries?" asked Arthur. And the answer came.

"An over-mighty king, brought low, cries out and shakes his chains."

Kai leapt up in passion. "Let's free him."

"No," roared Arthur. "We have another quest."

At his signal, we arose, overturning the tables. One-armed Bedwyr seized the Cauldron, heaving it upon a warrior's back. I seized the Horn. Another took the Salver and a third the Sword of the Enchanter. Grimly we fought our way to the palace door. The noise of battle brought our spearmen from the shore. Laughing we hewed our way to the ships and sprang aboard. The Treasures were ours.

But no. The warrior with the Sword had fallen. "Back," shouted Arthur, springing to the shore. We followed.

Before our eyes the meadows and the hall vanished. In their place reared up the glass fortress that we had seen at first. The six thousand silent warriors looked down. Swords and spears above our heads, we went to the assault and, as we charged, the crystal tower dissolved into a monstrous wave that fell upon us.

When I opened my eyes again, I was on board

40

Prydwen, drifting with the tide. Arthur was there, Kai, Bedwyr, Mightygrasp and two other warriors. Of the other ships and our comrades there was no sign.

The Treasures that had lured us to Annwn had vanished.

I made a song of this adventure and the last verse ended:

> *"Three shiploads we sailed to plunder Annwn*
> *Save seven, none returned with Arthur of sad*
> *memory."*

Arthur listened to all verses, pale-faced and wet-eyed. But when he heard the last two words his face flushed crimson. Leaping up he pointed to the door and I fled from his hall.

to win a bride

Arthur's anger was terrible, as the bear's. I slunk away and hid myself while the bards smirked in their beards. But like the bear's, our chieftain's anger did not last.

My song, which had roused his rage, flew from mouth to mouth and harp to harp. Before a year was out the fame of that ill-fated voyage spread through the land. The names of those who had perished beneath the waves were exalted. Far from shunning Arthur's hall, men came from Logres to the east, from as far as Pictland in the North, just to set eyes on the leader who feared nothing and no one in this or any other world. Fresh exploits waited, and did not wait for long.

One night a young warrior demanded entry to Kelliwic. When Mightygrasp and Kai would not let him in he threatened to make such a clamour folk would hear him in Ireland. The youth was Culhwych, Arthur's cousin, come to seek help to win Olwen, white as the swan, yellow-haired as the gorse flower, as his bride.

Olwen's father Ysbaddaden was a mighty man, savage and foul-tempered. With good reason, for it was foretold he would die the day his daughter married. When Culhwych asked for her hand, he set him forty tasks that he was sure were impossible. Culhwych knew better. With the aid of Arthur and his men, no task was too daunting.

Arthur's good humour returned. He sent out the call and tenscore men of fame flocked to Kelliwic, each with his special skill. One ran faster than any horse alive, another could walk along treetops without breaking a twig, a third could leap three hundred acres in one bound, a fourth could talk the language of the birds and beasts.

With their aid, nine and thirty tasks were light work.

But the last was not so easy. Ysbaddaden declared that to prepare him for the wedding feast he must have the magic razor, comb and scissors that sat between the ears of Twrch Trwyth, boar of boars, inside whose colossal body raged the soul of a dead king.

Only one man could handle the hound-pack to hunt him. And that was Mabon, son of Modron. But where was he to be found? He had been snatched from the cradle at birth. Since then no one had seen him.

"I'll find him," cried Kai.

"I'll go," said Bedwyr.

And with he who spoke the language of the birds and beasts, they set out.

the story of mabon

After many weary miles they found the Great Ousel, a wise and ancient bird, and asked her if she knew where Mabon was.

The Ousel said, "When I was young, I began to peck with my beak on an anvil. Now it is no bigger than a nut. Yet I never heard of him. But ask the Stag, who is older than me."

When they found the Stag, he told them, "See that rotting stump. When I was young, it was a seedling. I've seen it grow a mighty oak and die. But Mabon – I have heard nothing of him. Ask the Owl, who is my elder."

Said the Owl: "I've seen three forests grow and die here, but of Mabon I know not a thing. Go ask the Eagle, hatched long before me."

The Eagle preened its wings. "See that rock. That was a mountain on which I sat and pecked the stars. Now it is no more, but where Mabon is I never heard."

Kai and Bedwyr were in despair, but the Eagle said, "Only one creature is greater than me: the Mighty Salmon of Aber Henvelen."

They found the Mighty Salmon where the fresh water and salt mix.

He told them, "When I swim up the river, past the shining fortress, I hear a prisoner cry in despair. That is Mabon, son of Modron, held there since a child."

"We'll call up Arthur and his men and lay siege to Mabon's prison."

"Useless," said the Salmon. "There is one way only to attack the fortress. By water. Now climb on my back."

With Kai and Bedwyr on his shoulders, the Mighty Salmon swam up river till the shining fortress walls towered over them. From deep inside his dungeon Mabon cried aloud.

Kai answered. "Mabon. We are here to free you. Will your captors take ransom – gold or silver?"

"No," came the answer. "Only fighting can free me."

"Then we're your men," cried Kai. And with that he gave such a blow that the prison walls burst. Bedwyr took Mabon on his back and so they came back to Kelliwic in triumph.

In gratitude for freedom Mabon gladly agreed to hunt Twrch Trwyth. But it was not so simple.

"First I must have a special leash to hold the hounds. That leash can only be woven of hairs taken from Giant Dillus's beard. And those must be plucked with wooden tweezers while he is still alive."

"Let us go," said Kai to Bedwyr.

the story of giant dillus

They travelled till they saw smoke rising from a hill. Giant Dillus had killed a great pig and was roasting it whole for his supper. Said Kai cunningly, "Let him eat and fall asleep."

They waited till the giant's snores filled the air, then crept into his camp and dug a pit beneath him. Dillus's huge body slid down and stuck fast. Swiftly Kai plucked the beard out hair by hair. As he snatched the last one, Dillus awoke in pain and fury. But before he could clamber from the pit, Kai swung his great sword and Dillus lay dead.

how arthur insulted kai

All was now ready for the hunting of Twrch Trwyth. That night there was feasting at Kelliwic. Mead flowed like water. When they heard of Kai's trick the hall rang with laughter. Arthur, in high spirits, called me to him, snatched my harp and made up a song.

He taunted Kai for his cunning and sang, "If Dillus had been awake, he'd have been the death of you."

It was a rough jest. Kai took it for a mortal insult. Leaping from his seat, he marched from the hall. In the morning when the warriors gathered for the hunt, Kai had gone from Kelliwic.

Arthur bitterly cursed his heedless joke on his lifelong comrade. But there was nothing to be done, for Kai was nowhere to be found. More bitter news awaited Arthur. But that was still to come.

the story of twrch trwyth

The morning was cold and clear, mist clung to the grass, horses stamped the ground, hounds ran round yelping and warriors gathered for the hunt.

Arthur placed Bedwyr at one side, holding in his great hound Cabal, and Mabon, son of Modron, at the other, leading on the pack. Thus they ranged through the forests, the high land and the low. All kinds of game they raised, but not a sight of the mighty Twrch Trwyth, nor the seven young boars said to be with him. As the sun set and the hunt was called off for the day, a messenger brought news of the boar. He and his litter were ravaging the countryside across the sea in Ireland. Irish warriors pursued and fought with him in vain.

Next day Arthur's band took ship and joined the chase. So fast did the cunning savage boar and his brood run that only the fleetest heroes could keep pace with him. Every now and then he would turn at bay, goring and rending horse and man. Three days it lasted. On the first, the Irish fought him. On the second, Arthur's warband. And on the third, Arthur himself closed with his quarry – Boar against boar. But only one of the boar's litter died. Now Twrch Trwyth turned to the sea, plunged in, and, followed by his six remaining sons, swam over to Cornwall. Arthur followed swiftly in

47

Prydwen, hounding him up rivers and down. More of the young boars died, but so did Arthur's warriors.

Next day Twrch Trwyth was lost in the forest. Arthur called off his weary men and went back to Kelliwic. That evening the mead horn passed round, spirits rose again and the hall rang with pledges of great deeds when the hunt began next day. And the boasts found their answer in the heart of one young listener. Before night turned to dawn, Gwydre stole out to mingle with the huntsmen, unseen by his father. Eagerly he rode forth, but did not ride home. For when Twrch Trwyth was brought to bay on the shores of Aber Henvelen, Arthur's son was one of eight men killed. His body drifted out with the tide and was never found.

All this was unknown to Arthur. He and his huntsmen in full cry followed Twrch Trwyth across the river mouth and on to the farther shore.

There Arthur caught him – a giants' struggle. The mighty boar was rolled back into the water. Mabon, son of Modron, snatched the razor from the bristles of his head. Another took the scissors.

As the light died, Arthur's spear gave Twrch Trwyth a fatal thrust. The sea ran red as the boar vanished from the hunter's sight. But in that moment Bedwyr reached out his arm and snatched the comb.

The quest for Culhwych's bride, Olwen, was over.

how kai
proved himself

The joy of the wedding was like the sun shining a
moment in the sky before the dark clouds of gloom hung
over Kelliwic again. Arthur mourned Gwydre and with
pride, for he had died a hero's death, facing the giant
boar, spear in hand.

Losing one son, Arthur made the more of Amr, his
chosen successor. His third son, brave, silent, Llachau,
he scarcely seemed to see. To add to his burden, Kai, the
comrade of his youth, had gone, none knew where. At
night in the hall men ate and drank in silence. I kept my
mouth closed and my harp quiet.

Worse was to come. Twrch Trwyth had his revenge.
Word came from Wales that his mate, Henwen, was
rampaging through the land. None could stop her, none
could catch her, none could lay her low. As she ranged
the hills and dales, news came of marvels. Here and there
the old sow gave birth, but not to pigs, men said: to
swarms of bees, an eagle and wolf cubs.

There was more, and fearful too. Near the sea that lies
between Wales and Ireland she gave birth to a young cat.
Now Henwen vanished in the forests and the strange

offspring was thrown into the sea for fear of harm. But it did not drown. It swam like an otter. It landed on the sacred island of Mona, and Palugh's sons, who lived there, pulled it from the sea. They gave it shelter and food. But soon it grew until it needed no nourishment from them. Palugh's cat began to hunt, first beasts, then men. It grew by what it ate.

Its hair was coarse as gorse, its teeth were long as walrus tusks, its eyes were big and glowed like brass cauldrons. The strength of a lion matched with the greed of hounds. Nigh on two hundred men fell to its claws. The land was gripped in fear.

At first Arthur, in the depths of his sorrow, did nothing. But at last he roused himself, called for arms and horses, told his men to ready themselves to ride and do battle with the monstrous beast. The war-band set out but rode no further than ten miles. On the road before us, we saw a tall warrior approaching on horseback. His clothes were travel-stained, his face weary, his hair uncombed, his spear-tip red with blood.

As he came near, we saw with wonder the huge black cat's head hanging from his saddle.

"Kai," the word flew from Arthur's lips.

Kai rode on to Kelliwic, but as he passed, he threw the head of Palugh's cat at Arthur's feet.

arthur's reckless vow

Time heals all hurts, but not time spent remembering. Arthur took heart and drove his troubles from him by deeds of prowess and valour. His fame spread from coast to coast. The bravest warriors came to serve him, to follow him, to fight where he led.

With Bedwyr to make peace between them, Arthur and Kai rode side by side again. They were comrades once more, though the days of quick laughter were behind them. Kai was not easy in himself. Arthur's might and wealth, rising with his fame, were outgrowing Kelliwic. Our chief began to look abroad and think of building a new, a greater hall to fit his dreams.

I saw all this but thought little of it. All seemed as it should be. One day Arian asked me: "Will you be happier in a grander palace far from here where the gods are happy?"

"Why not?" I answered. "With Arthur anything is possible. As he rises, I shall rise — all of us shall rise."

"And fall?" she asked.

I laughed, but her words stayed in my thoughts.

Each night at Arthur's command I sang of chiefs and

heroes from the past. His favourite was Bran, god-king who led the armies of the Island of the Mighty across the sea, walking before his fleet. Bran's warriors crossed an uncrossable river, marching on his back.

"He who is a chief let him be a bridge," I sang. And always Arthur made me sing the words a second and a third time.

When Bran was slain, seven warriors bore home his head. For he had commanded them, "Bury my head on the White Mount, its face towards the sea. In this way no plague will ever come into the Island."

Those final words raised Arthur to his feet. All looked at him in amazement as he said:

"The defence of this island is the task of live heroes, not buried heads. Tomorrow I shall send to the White Mount and dig up the Head of Bran. My arms alone shall protect these shores."

Fear gripped my heart. I remembered the words of Lailoken, mad prophet of the forest: "Buried kings will be dug from their graves. The Island will be drenched in tears." I looked around and saw Morgaine. She was always first to urge Arthur to any deed, no matter how reckless. Now she gazed at him in silence.

Before another seven days had passed, the deed was done. Henceforth, Arthur's valour would be our island's only shield.

part three

red dragon,
white dragon

a mysterious stranger

Before the blackthorn turned red, Arthur's pledge was put to the test. The ships of the Saxons, people of the White Dragon, swooped on our shores like birds of prey. Swiftly they came, swiftly they went. All that reached Arthur's hall were the cries of the widows and the grievous complaints of the farmers for slaughtered cattle and crops in flames.

Arthur called in his war-band. We rode light, each warrior with two swift-footed spearmen running by his side. We rode by night, taking our food where we could. Hither and thither we rode, as the tidings reached us, crossing the land of other lords, whether they liked it or not.

The first time there was only the stench of charred wood and flesh to greet us. The second time we saw their sails dip below the line where the sky meets water. But the third time we caught them, carousing. Only a lucky few reached their boats. Three nights without ceasing we feasted, sharing the booty we had taken. Arthur kept nothing for himself but the helmet of the Saxon leader to drink his mead from. I sang:

"I was with Arthur where bright water ran red
Like a wild boar, he gave ravens their food."

That winter there was peace. Folk worked in the fields and the shore-watchers looked out on an empty sea. Spring turned to summer, the oak put out its second leaves, frost came, then snow. All was quiet and Arthur grew restless again. As the year turned again to spring and the fires of Beltane burned, a strange thing happened. I did not understand its meaning then. I did not know that from this moment on we should see nothing but change.

An old man came to Kelliwic. His white hair hung on the shoulders of his robe, which was black as a crow. He would not give his name but he had the presence of a Druid, a holy man of the Old Law. With him was a young man in threadbare brown, a face of great beauty and clear blue eyes. He was called Cedwyn. He followed the New Law and wore a Christian cross around his neck.

Both cured the sick, the old one by laying on hands, the younger one with herbs and ointments. They were like travellers heading for different distant points who had found themselves together on the way. There was an air of wonder about the two and I could not take my eyes off them.

Then, one day, I knew the old man's face again. It was that of Lailoken, the mad warrior I had met in the

Northern woods. Yet when I spoke to him he did not know me. Mystery upon mystery.

Some great thing was to happen, I knew. And soon it came.

merlin

One evening at supper the old man rose in his place. All ceased their eating and their talking. But he spoke only to Arthur.

"Chieftain. You boast of your victories over the White Dragon. Yet they are boys' fights compared with what is to come."

Arthur flushed red, but mastered himself.

"Who are you, old man, and what is to come – if you truly know?"

"First my message, then my name. I know what is to come for a hundred, a thousand years, when you will be a memory and your warriors heaps of bones. Even now the White Dragon ravages the North – not ten shiploads but a hundred."

Arthur answered with a laugh.

"Then the hosts of Rheged and Gododdin and Efrawg must drive them out. They do not need me to save them."

There was some laughter around the hall.

"Fools," thundered the old man. "The Saxons are not come to plunder. They come to drive the men of Britain from their lands, to ravish their daughters. They will seize the Island of the Mighty."

"Do you prophesy, old man?" asked Arthur.

"No, I warn. Unless a war leader arises, the Red Dragon will go down and the White will triumph."

"And who is that leader?"

"He who raises the Sword of the Enchanter and smites the invader."

Arthur looked round quietly at Morgaine, who sat close by. Her eyes glowed, but she said nothing. Arthur spoke.

"The Sword of the Enchanter lies beneath the waves of Annwn beyond the sea."

"No," answered the old man. "The Sword of the Enchanter, which some call Kaledfwlch and some Caliburn, is close at hand. I can bring you to it – if you pledge to free the Island from its foes."

Morgaine was on her feet, about to speak, but the old man silenced her.

"Who will refuse Arthur the Sword of the Enchanter to free the Island of the Mighty?"

Now Arthur rose. "I will do it. But now, old man. Tell me your name."

"I am Merlin," was the answer.

sword from
the water

Between the forest and the sea lay a pool shadowed by rocks, ringed by reeds, deep and dark.

At dawn next day, when the mist coiled white over the water, we came to the shore. Arthur pale and stern, Merlin hooded and robed like night. Merlin's companion, Cedwyn, was nowhere to be seen. This was a time for the Old Law and he had nothing to do here. I stood on the rocks above, holding the horses' bridles and watching, for I knew I should see a wonder.

As the sun touched the treetops above the mist with yellow fire, Merlin raised his arms, old and gnarled as an oak branch, towards the sky and began to speak in a tongue older than ours. Arthur's eyes, wide as a child's, looked on the glassy surface of the lake.

Moments passed. Merlin spoke louder. Nothing happened. His voice faltered, his arms began to sink.

A whispering sound reached my ears. The faintest ripples kissed the reeds, as they spread from the middle of the lake. Above them the mist parted, a sunbeam flashed and answering fire came from the air above the water. Silver-blue in the morning gleamed the sword-blade that rose from the depths, then a thousand points sparkled on the jewelled hilt. A white arm, slender and curved, followed; white-clad shoulders, a head with hair of brilliant red, a lovely maiden, sword held aloft, walked on the pool as if it had been stone.

I held my breath. It was Arian and yet I knew it was not. As she came closer Arthur's arms raised, stretched out, the sword was passed to him and the maiden vanished into the lake again.

Caliburn, the Sword of the Enchanter, was now Arthur's. Now the battle for the Island of the Mighty must begin.

arian's warning

From that day on, Merlin never moved from Arthur's side, walking with him, seated alone with him or at table in the crowded hall. And Arthur listened and heeded. Plans were hatched, orders given, everything was changing. Arthur talked no more with Kai or Bedwyr. Morgaine was not to be seen.

My days were passed with Cedwyn. He was of my age and better company than Amr the proud, or shy

Llachau. I watched him in wonder – his constant praying on his knees in quiet corners, his reading and writing. He ate nothing but bread and wild cress, drank only water, slept on the ground even when the frost was white. He had no vanity. His hair was rough cut as though he'd sheared himself. I offered to cut it straight for him, but he only shook his head. The New Law had strange ways.

When I went to the maze house, I found Arian cold and strange. I asked her what was wrong.

"With me, nothing. With you, a great deal. You and your lord play with the New Law."

"But Merlin is not of the New law," I began to say. She shook her head.

"Merlin has one foot in the sea and one on shore. You and your lord will regret it all one day."

how arthur plunged his sword into stone

Another winter passed before Arthur and Merlin judged the time was right to move. Then move they did from Kelliwic to Caerleon, on the River Usk, the place men called the City of the Legions.

The Roman legions were long departed across the

sea, but their power and glory lingered after them. Mighty walls of dressed stone encircled palaces, temples and baths. Roads and aqueducts marched in the air on arches. Statues to the gods, to the Thunderer, to Nodens Silverhand, Llud of the lightning strike, Epona of the horses, towered over us. Some buildings were as new. Some were decayed, owls nested in their roofs. But the place swarmed like an upset hive, folk by the thousand.

At first it seemed madness to me, to leave Kelliwic's timbered warmth for these high halls as cold as tombs. But soon I saw what Arthur or, to speak truth, what Merlin was after. With the Spring Festival, chieftains and their war-bands began to gather from every corner of the land. They rode in high and proud, armed and mailed, and none more grand than the great ones of the North, the Lords of Rheged and Gododdin, with their sons and warriors.

If they were grand, then Arthur, appearing before the throng in the Forum – the vast pillared square where once the legions tramped – Arthur was magnificent, his mail-coat glistening like a golden fish's scales.

Merlin mounted the steps below the pillars and spoke to the silent crowd.

"Men of Britain, warriors of Bran's Island, Land of the Mighty. We stand in peril from the White Dragon. Its ravening hordes destroy the treasures of our realm. And they are unending. Beat them back once and they will come again. Only crushing defeat can banish them.

Only if all join together in one host. One host needs one war leader, one Pendragon. I call on you to follow the chosen one, Uther's son, Arthur, the Boar of Cornwall, holder of the Sword."

As he said these words, Arthur drew his sword, Caliburn, from its scabbard. A sheet of flame like lightning split the air. A great cheer filled the Forum.

"Approach," called Merlin. "Swear on the Sword to follow Arthur."

"Wait!" thundered the Lord of Gododdin. "Before you rush to follow Arthur. What is this – Uther's son? Arthur was born out of wedlock! Uther and Ygerna had two daughters after they were married. *Their* sons, Mordred and Gawain, are in our ranks today."

Merlin replied calmly, "Arthur is the son of Ygerna. And Uther is the father. If they lay together before their marriage, Arthur is still the son."

"We know that old story," roared Gododdin. "Let those believe it who choose. I choose not to."

He and the Lord of Rheged turned away with their following. The crowd began to make way for them. Merlin nodded to Arthur who sprang forward, Caliburn in his hand. All stood amazed as he swung the Sword, brilliant, through the air and buried it to its hilt in the stone base of a pillar.

"Bastard or not, I can pluck out that sword. Let he who can do the same show me and I will follow him. Let those who cannot, step up and swear on the hilt to join my host."

There was a moment's deep silence before Arthur reached forward and drew out the Sword from the pillar. Then came a great rush forward as chiefs and warriors came to swear to Arthur as Pendragon. But Rheged and Gododdin paused a moment and called out, "We do not yield to tricks." Followed by their warriors, they marched from the square.

gawain and mordred

A great open tent of red- and gold-striped silk was thrown up in the Forum. There in the morning sunshine Arthur sat on his couch. Chieftains came to speak with him, to pledge numbers of men, to agree to be there when he raised his standard. I looked on and thought: The Boar is king in all but name.

Yet Arthur was troubled. He bent and listened as Merlin whispered in his ear. I knew what they were saying – were these warriors enough to go to war without the Lords of Rheged and Gododdin?

As I watched, two young men, princes by their dress, came into the pavilion and saluted Arthur. I knew them. Mordred, son of Anna, Gawain, son of Gwyar. Both were

63

handsome, in their different ways, Mordred dark and severe as winter, Gawain fair and open as summer. Arthur greeted them warmly. Whatever men said about his birth, they were his sisters' sons.

Gawain spoke, his voice light and courteous.

"Rheged and Gododdin will not join you. But we and our men will."

A great smile lightened Arthur's face as if a cloud passed. He rose and embraced them both.

Next day the fields outside the city rang to the clash of arms as warriors showed their strength and skill. And none more so than Gawain. He had a way with men. With a smile or a word he could make them follow and obey. He was like the sun warming all around him.

Merlin told Arthur, "Make him your Penteulu, your Captain of Captains." Arthur nodded – his mind was already fixed on it.

With Gawain came his younger brother, slightly built, with the face and hands of a girl, yet the spirit of a lion. Kai mocked him, nicknamed him Fairhands. But when Gareth wanted to avenge the insult, Gawain coaxed him out of his anger.

"A jest, Gareth. That is Kai's way. Tomorrow or the next day he will see how wrong he is. Let us fight the foe, not each other."

Others had their eyes on Gareth. The day before we marched, proud Amr and shy Llachau came to Arthur.

"Let us ride with you, Father."

At once Arthur, his eye on Amr, began to say, "Not yet, you..."

But Amr countered. "Gareth is no older than me."

Arthur said nothing, but only nodded.

amr's death

As we rode out of Caerleon, the Saxon boats sailed into havens on our distant coasts. First they fought the Lords of Rheged and Gododdin, threw them back, then sailed to the south, ravaging as they went. Bold with success, they turned and headed for Deva that lies between the North and South. Their intent was clear: to cut the land in two. Near Ercing we surprised them at the sacking of a town and where the sun shone red on the river we took and held the vital ford.

Sustained by Morgaine's promise of protection, I fought and sang. Kai laughed and pointed. "Not a scratch on him!"

As the next day dawned, both armies faced each other on the field, we on the high ground. Gawain marshalled our ranks, the spearmen in circles like hedgehogs, warriors dismounted forming wedges to split the enemy ranks.

Arthur raised the Red Dragon standard, they the White. He unsheathed Caliburn, the lightning dazzled them. What a thunder of sword-hilts on shields. What an onrush of gold-torqued heroes, what a trampling of blood-stained cloth. Men fell like rushes cut down.

When the tumult of fighting, the screams of the wounded, were at their height, the White Dragon warriors tried to break our line and escape. A handful of our men, dizzy and maddened by the din, lost their courage, turned and ran. Like a bear in his fury, Arthur was among them, blade swinging. One, two went down, the rest turned back, shamed into bravery. The line held once more.

As the sun set on the rout of the White Dragon, men carried the body of Amr to Arthur's tent. He had been one of those who had broken and run. Llachau, who had fought like a prince, came to his father to share his sorrow.

But Arthur rebuffed him saying, "You are alive, he is dead."

Kai put an arm around Llachau's shoulder and led him away.

That night I sang of Amr and his tragedy, while the warriors crowding round listened in silence.

> *"A father's hand, unknowing*
> *Cut him down."*

66

Arthur's face was like thunder. Gawain looked at me and slowly shook his head. Without words he told me Arthur knew it was Amr when he struck him down.

gathering the armies

Our triumph was just for a moment. The White Dragon was wounded, but not dead. We fought him again, and yet again. Six more battles we fought, on sea dunes, in marshes, by river crossings and on hilltops. The Red Dragon streamed in the breeze. Caliburn was unsheathed with terrifying flame. Our losses were many. I sang of the heroes who slept with the light in their eyes, mail-coats washed with blood, returning to earth, short lives, long grieving for their folk.

When all hung in the balance, Hywel, Arthur's cousin, came with his men from Little Britain across the sea and threw their weight in the scales. At our seventh encounter the Saxons were penned in the woods. We circled them round and about, denied them food and water. After many days they begged for quarter. Arthur was stern. They could leave with their lives – if they pledged never again to land on our shores. The words were given. The White Dragon sails vanished to the east and we went home in triumph.

Arian welcomed me again. I teased her for her doubts of Merlin and his shadow, Cedwyn.

"All goes well," I exulted. "The gods smile."

"Which gods?" she asked, with her keen glance.

"What does it matter, if they smile?"

"You will see," she told me.

She saw further than me. But I saw some things that gave cause for thought. Arthur had Cedwyn with him, talking and praying. This did not surprise me. He was brooding and guilty now that Amr lay beneath the turf at Ercing. A mourner takes comfort where he can.

But Arthur was not brooding only over Amr. With another spring came desperate news. The ships of the White Dragon had been sighted yet again. In great numbers. This time, men said, they came not just with warriors but with kings, with families and with cattle. They came to make our land their home.

Arthur was like no other man. The greater the danger, the greater his daring. Right or wrong, he did not hesitate. He called first Mordred, then Cedwyn to him. They met in secret. Pledges were made. Mordred rode away on his war-horse, Cedwyn on his old mule. They were away a long time, while Arthur paced his hall like a trapped lion.

One summer day they came back to Caerleon, when war-bands thronged the Forum. With Mordred came the

Lords of Rheged and Gododdin, at their back the hosts of the North. With Cedwyn came Bishop Dyfrig and a double line of brown monks bearing white crosses.

Before the multitude of armed men, Dyfrig took a tabard of rich silks, inlaid with a silver cross, and placed it over Arthur's shoulders. He spoke in the tongue of the Romans who brought this god to our shores.

Beside me Cedwyn, eyes shining, whispered, "One Chieftain over all, One God over all."

"What if men do not worship this god?" I asked.

"Let them worship as they please. The One God made all," he answered.

Dyfrig took next a scroll, painted with the face of a beautiful woman with round, upturned eyes.

"The Mother of God." Cedwyn's whisper was no more than a breath.

"Then she made him," I muttered.

He did not hear me. A shout like thunder burst over our ears as Rheged, Gododdin and their men swore on the Sword to follow Arthur into battle with the White Dragon.

That night in the hall when mead and wine ran like a flood, Arthur called to me and I struck my harp. "I sing to the Lord of Heaven and Earth, ruler of every kin."

When dawn was on the distant hills I staggered into the half-dark streets. Arian rose before me like a ghost. "The mead was strong. Taliesin praises the new god."

I answered with bravado. "I sing to who promises

69

victory for the Red Dragon. I am Arthur's man. Let those who are offended strike me down."

A voice spoke from the shadows. I knew it was Morgaine. "No, your fate is not to die, Little One. Sing your song, live on, even when you would rather die."

the white dragon beaten

And so to war again. We fought four battles under the Christian Cross and the Red Dragon and the emblem of She who made All. Four times we drove the White Dragon warriors to their ships. Four times they dragged themselves away, then, sailing to another haven, fell on our shores like the plague.

But then at Badon Hill we snared them. And with a great shout fell upon them. Those who broke and ran struggled to the seashore. But hidden in the Saxon ships were country folk with club and billhook. Such a revenge they took for every ravaging that no invader escaped.

The slaughter at Badon told us we should have peace for a generation. Rheged, Gododdin, every lord and his men rode away to their own realms, the name of Arthur on their lips. Gawain the gentle, Gareth Fairhands and the silent Mordred stayed, as did many a young hero. For where Arthur went was adventure and glory.

We rode to Caerleon. There was feasting, the making of speeches and boasts – to be fulfilled another day. But all heard in silence when Arthur told of his three pledges, made in the darkest hour.

One was to drive the White Dragon from the Island of the Mighty. That was done. The second was to build in lands newly gained to the east of Cornwall a newer, finer hall, of timber from the forests and dressed stone from the ruins of cities. And the third was to ask Ogvran the Mighty for his daughter as wife.

Ogvran's daughter Guanhumara, or Guinevere as they called her in Little Britain, for she was known across the sea, was the fairest of women. So fair was she that by ancient law and hidden powers she was the Spirit of the Realm. Only the greatest might seek her as wife. But who was now greater than Arthur?

Merlin said nothing, though the look in his eye told me that this notion had not come from him. But who could say no to Arthur now, in the hour of victory?

Yet something weighed on Arthur's mind. He called me, speaking low: "Morgaine has gone. Go secretly to Kelliwic and find her. This troubles me."

As the leaves turned red-gold in the woods, I rode to Kelliwic. Only guards and servants sat and diced in the quiet hall. And the House of the Maze was deserted.

I roamed its corridors, calling softly. By some chance I found my way to Morgaine's chamber, where I once found my true voice.

It was empty. Dry leaves rustled on the floor, which echoed to my tread.

Of Morgaine and Arian there was no sign. They had vanished into the air.

When I returned to tell Arthur, "Morgaine is gone," a cloud seemed to pass over his face. Then he said, "No, we shall meet again."

I knew that would be so, but it brought me no comfort.

part four

camelot in its glory

lancelot

I had no time to think what I had lost. With a little space for the healing of wounds and the sharpening of swords, we went to war again.

Arthur's host took ship and sailed southward over the sea to Little Britain. Hywel, his cousin, who had come to his aid against the White Dragon, was now hard-pressed by foes from Gaul. And Arthur paid his debts.

We sailed, we rode, we marched. We fell like a torrent on Hywel's enemies. At the sight of our banners they fled. The monks rejoiced in the power of the New Law. But I knew that Arthur's name was like a thousand armed men, turning the guts of the opposing armies to water.

As a spear thrown in the air reaches its greatest height, so Arthur's fame reached its zenith. As we conquered, I knew that Arthur would never again lead his warriors into battle – against an enemy. To know the future and be powerless to prevent it is a crushing burden. Morgaine had warned me that I should pay for every gift I had.

I knew that our lives were changed for ever. For in the clash of battle Arthur noticed one of Hywel's warriors, his red armour like a flame, his sword invincible. When the fighting was done, Hywel brought the young man to Arthur's tent. We saw he was as handsome as he was brave. Even Gawain must yield first place to him.

He knelt to Arthur as to a king and begged him, "Take me back with you to the Island of the Mighty. Let me serve you."

Arthur looked at Hywel, who smiled and nodded.

"Will you leave home and kin?" he asked the young man. A shadow crossed the fair face. "I have no kin – my father was killed. As a babe in arms I last saw my mother."

"But who reared you, trained you for war?"

"I did."

All looked in wonder, and none more awe-struck than Merlin, as a tall woman appeared. I knew her face and family, not of the earth but of the water.

"This is my foster child found by the shore, reared in my realm. His sword, his horse, he got from me. I give him to you, Arthur. He will find adventure and fame with you."

"What is his name?"

"Lancelot of the Lake."

the round table

We sailed home to a realm of peace and ease. Country folk gathered in their harvest without fear, the land resounded with Arthur's praise. None had more renown than he.

To match that fame he called the finest craftsmen to build him a fortress to the east in Logres, as he had pledged to do. From the warm southern seas timber was brought and carved exquisitely; from the hills of the West great blocks of stone. A mighty home for a mighty warrior.

He chose a hill where the stream called Cam flows, and called it Camelot. Three ramparts ringed it round. No host could storm it while its defenders manned its walls.

This hall like a palace with its blue-gold hangings, its trophies and ornaments, was so huge his whole war-band could gather there. When the mead horn passed around and I tuned my harp and Arthur took his place on the fleece-lined couch, there was a rough grandeur never seen in our history since the ancient days. To be there was fortune.

But to be near to Arthur was a boon. The seat next to

him had stayed empty since Amr was buried. None took it, though I saw Mordred stand by it as if to say, "No one *else* shall sit there."

There was a jostling for the nearer seats of honour, the heroes' places. At first it was like a boy's game, then came impatience, next anger – bread crusts were thrown, wine bowls scattered, fists shaken, blows struck, and last, swords drawn. Kai with his angry strictness, Gawain with his soothing words, Lancelot with good humour, parted the fighters, shoved them back, settled the order. Arthur frowned in silence. But the harmony of the feast was broken.

One day as we walked in the woods we met a tall fellow in carpenter's apron, toolbag at his shoulder. He spoke to Arthur, man to man. "A ruler such as you should have peace in his hall. Peace comes when each knows his place and is sure of it."

"What does that mean, good man?" asked Arthur.

"Just this. I will build you a table such as has never been seen before, where your choice warriors will sit, none having higher rank than the other! I will make it so large that all have room, yet so small that when you travel you may take it with you."

"What table can this be?"

"Why, a table like the circle of the heavens. A table so marvellous its name will last as long as your fame. Men will tell of Arthur's Round Table for ever."

"Then make it, man, make it. You shall have the

payment you desire," urged Arthur.

"Payment," answered the carpenter in contempt. "None can pay for this table. They can only deserve it. Its power will last while its owner's merit lasts. Only fatal quarrels can break its unity."

With that the carpenter vanished in the trees. Arthur was bewildered. He did not see through Merlin's disguise as I did.

guinevere

The Round Table took its place in Camelot's hall. Twenty-four chosen, tried and tested heroes had their seats – only death or disgrace could deny them.

Now all was accord in Camelot. The time was ripe for the redeeming of his third pledge – to marry Guinevere, Spirit of the Realm. Messengers rode to Hen Dinas with lavish gifts and in time rode back. Her answer was yes and her father added his consent. None could say no to Arthur in those days.

Who was to ride to Mighty Ogvran Vawr's great fortress and bring his daughter home to Camelot? Men waited on Arthur's word. He chose not Kai, not Bedwyr, not even noble Gawain, but the new warrior, Lancelot.

Kai was angry. He was the senior, hero of battles fought when Lancelot was in his cradle. Gawain only smiled – he had no drop of envy in his blood. Besides, he loved Lancelot as a brother.

Who put it into Arthur's head to do it? Merlin? I looked into the sage's face and knew the answer was no. Arthur had decided and no man could go against his word. Kai kept his anger to himself but it did not die. Only loyalty, which meant more than life to him, kept him silent.

So Lancelot, bold in his scarlet armour, rode out, a hundred gold-torqued warriors at his back. And as the fires of Beltane burned and those of the New Law celebrated Pentecost, Lancelot rode up the hill to Camelot with Guinevere at his side – a man and a maid so handsome that crowds cheered and smiled to see them.

When she dismounted and he led her up to Arthur, I saw my chief all at once with new eyes – he like a grizzled bear, she like a large-eyed doe. She knelt to him. Beaming, he raised her up. But as her arm rested on his she gave one fleeting glance, quick as a bird's wing, towards her escort. Of a thousand on the spot, I was the only one who saw it.

Never, even in the days of Bran, was there a feast like that when Arthur married his Guinevere. The cattle and the sheep were slaughtered, boars and deer brought in from the chase, birds of the forest and farmyard, more than one can number, wine and mead flowed in torrents.

Arthur's bride was not only fair, she was stately, queenly and gracious.

When she rose from the table to offer Gawain as Penteulu, chief of all the war-bands, his horn of liquor, all rose with her and shouted aloud. All saw her as a marvel – none so beautiful had been seen before. Arthur looked on his young wife with pride.

But there was one a little way from her in the crowd who gazed at her as if no one else was present and they were alone together. Lancelot, he whom the Lady of the Lake had reared and armed. I saw and in a flash my eye turned to Merlin. He saw too. In that instant our eyes met and fell away. We understood one another.

But what is a single shadow in the brilliant light of day? The feasting went on, three days and three nights. I sang the beauty of Guinevere, the nobility of Arthur, the heroism of his warriors, until my voice growled in my throat.

Then we took horses and rode, first to Kelliwic in the West, then north to Carluel where the Legions built the wall and last of all returning to the splendid hall at Camelot. We feasted through the year, through all the festivals, with the new names the New Law gave them – Christmas, Pentecost, Lammas.

On the hills the fires of Beltane and Samhain still blazed but the New Law ruled. Yet if there was a gloomy face at our feasting it was the monk Cedwyn. I put my arm about his shoulder and bid him rejoice with his fellow man.

He replied in earnest anger: "The proud, the idle, all they do when not at war is eat, drink and sleep. They scorn the humble who bring their food to them."

I told him, "They have earned their mead. Their pride is paid for on the field of battle. They earned the peace that all rejoice in. They will be immortal for their deeds."

"Immortal?" said Cedwyn. "Only these?" He pointed to the crowded, noisy benches. "I tell you, every one who breathes shall live for ever. God has promised."

"What, every one?" I teased him. "Where will He put all those souls? Heaven will be crowded out."

He smiled and shook his head, then went outside to his bed under the stars.

a golden age

Years of peace, years of plenty. It was a golden age. Arthur rode no more to war with gold-torqued warriors at his back. Caliburn stayed in its sheath, the flash of its blade no longer struck terror into the hearts of men. He grew more grand, seated on his white fleece-covered couch, or in the high-backed chair at the Table when his twenty-four chosen warriors gathered around him.

His exploits were our legend, but he loved to hear me sing the feats, the adventures of others. He could not bear to sit down, to eat, until he heard of some new deed, some fantastic tale. And once he had supped no one dared leave his place till Arthur rose.

New days, new manners. Guinevere was surrounded by maidens in silks and ribbons. Their words, their glances changed the ways of men. Peace had its arts as well as war.

Gawain and Lancelot excelled at them with wit and charm. But Kai grew uneasy and irritable with the new ways. I heard him dispute with Gawain one day.

"Our young men grow more like women – they think of nothing but the clothes on their backs. None of them has got the strength to throw a spear. Peace eats the sinews."

Gawain laughed. "Ah, but the grass grows greener when war ceases. Country folk are content, the land grows richer."

The New Law ruled. Bishops and monks came and went, and never went empty-handed. Gifts of money and land flowed from Arthur's hand. I sang the old songs, told the old stories. Arthur liked them best. I veiled their meanings, the lore of the old gods I hid behind cunning words.

But I could not refrain from taunting the solemn monks poring over their parchments:

> *"Do books know where the tide flows from?*
> *Why night follows day?*
> *What makes evil, what makes good?*
> *Why one thorn is white, the other red?"*

I debated with Cedwyn when no one else could hear us and mistake our meaning. Said he, "I love the woods, the rivers and the trees but I do not worship them. I worship God who made everything. He is everywhere."

"A god without a home?" I asked him, and he smiled.

So the years went by in splendour at Arthur's Camelot. New ways, new manners and a new god. But beyond the ramparts in the distant dark forests, deep lakes and mist-girt marshes, other spirits watched and waited.

green challenger

One New Year's Day Arthur stood by his place and looked around the crowded, noisy hall. He waited with all the eagerness of a boy till everyone was served. That was his rule. At last he sat down and still he would not eat, but waited. For it was his rule also not to put knife into meat till he had heard some marvellous and untold tale.

The moments passed but no one spoke. Men looked at each other, then looked away. Silence grew deeper, deep as the snow that lay around Camelot.

A chilly blast of air blew through the hall. Torch flames guttered as the great doors burst open and a horseman rode in, to stop a spear's-length from Arthur and Guinevere, amid the awe-struck guests.

He was a giant, huge as his horse. His long hair hung down from his head to his waist. In one hand he bore a holly branch, and in the other a mountainous battle-axe. More wonderful, the rider and horse, clothes, hair, harness, everything, were glittering green.

"Who is your chief?" he thundered as his red eyes rolled.

"I am he," said Arthur. "Come down and join us at our feast. Or are you here to challenge us to combat?"

"Ha. If I were here to fight, none here could match me. But you see I wear no armour. I'm here for sport."

"What sport?"

The green warrior raised his axe. "Let some man here strike me a blow with this axe – if they dare – and in a year from today, accept a blow from me."

No one moved. This challenge was not of the mortal earth. Arthur stood up. "Give me the axe." The huge green man dismounted, holding out the fearful blade to Arthur. But Gawain was on his feet.

"No, let me strike the blow – and clear the debt in a year's time."

The stranger looked down. "Who are you?"

"I am Gawain. Tell me where I may find you."

Smiling grimly, he answered, "First strike off my head, then I'll tell."

Gawain raised the axe. Its razor edge glinted in the light, struck down, a true blow. The green head bounced among the shrinking feet of the guests.

They sat amazed as the weird warrior strode forward, seized the head and mounted his horse again, turning it to the door.

Then the head, held aloft, spoke:

"Gawain, meet me in one year's time, at the Green Chapel."

And he was gone, out into the winter's air.

the story of gawain's quest

The year passed. No one spoke again of what had happened, but all thought of Gawain's fate. And when the smoke rose from Samhain's fires, one and all rode down the hill from Camelot to give him a hero's farewell.

"What can I do but dare?" he said, and spurred his horse to the north.

For more than fifty days and nights he journeyed, through mountain, forest, marshland and moor, fighting wild beasts and worse. At night he lay in charcoal burners' huts or on the very ground, frozen in his cloak. Yet he found no one who knew the Green Chapel.

But there came a day when, through the trees, a stronghold sprang into view, mighty amid its palisades, towers gleaming with light. As if he were expected, gates swung open, servants took his horse, helped him shed his rusty armour, led him to a blessed blazing fire.

The lord, a powerful, laughing, red-faced man, greeted him. When he heard Gawain's name, he roared. "Good fortune to have so famed a guest."

When Gawain had bathed and changed his clothes, they sat down to eat. Two ladies entered. Gawain rose. One was old and stately with a withered face. The other, the lord's wife, spring to her winter, lovely to look at. Without delay she sat at Gawain's side and spoke with him cheerfully.

Three days passed in feasting, song and dance. His host's wife paid Gawain every attention.

But New Year's Day approached and Gawain said that he must go.

"Why?" urged his host. "What errand is so pressing that you must leave us?"

Gawain told him. "I have a tryst that I must keep, at the Green Chapel – and I do not know where it lies."

"Then rest easy. It is but an hour's ride from here. You shall stay with us three days more."

"You are a generous host."

"Ha. We shall have sport. Tomorrow I go hunting.

You rest on your bed."

"What sport is that?"

"See, we will exchange. I'll give you what I win by hunting, if you give me whatever you gain here."

Gawain laughed. "A bargain. But you'll get little of it."

The host laughed. "We shall see."

As the horns blew in the morning, Gawain lay asleep. But not alone. The door to his chamber opened and closed again. His host's wife sat beside him on the bed. He tried to rise. She held him down. "Any maid would envy me – having Gawain, the world's lover, as my prisoner." She smiled. "But are you Gawain?"

"Why?"

"You haven't tried to kiss me."

"As my lady commands," he said. They kissed.

That evening the host returned, with slaughtered deer. "Here is what I gained," he said. "Now you." Gawain laughed, and kissed him once.

On the second day the lord went hunting again and his wife came again to Gawain's bedside. "Teach me the game of love," she whispered. "You know more than me," he answered.

That night his host brought a great boar killed in the hunt. Gawain gave him two kisses.

The third day began as the others. The lady asked Gawain with a frown: "Do you have a love who pleases you more?"

"Not yet," he said.

"You are cruel." She left his side. "Can I have a keepsake from you?" she asked.

"I have nothing to give, I fear."

She took off a green sash from her dress. "Accept this from me."

"I cannot – I have nothing I can give you."

"Take it," she urged, "it will protect you from any blow." In that moment he thought of the Green Chapel and he took the girdle from her.

That night he accepted the gift of a fox, and kissed his host three times, but said nothing of the girdle he had gained. Then he said goodbye and thanked him for his kindness.

In the snowy dawn a servant led Gawain through the moors to the edge of a ravine but would go no further. "Sir, do not go on. You will die for sure. Go back where you came from. I'll keep your secret."

Gawain shook his head. "I cannot take the coward's way."

"Farewell, then." The servant spurred his horse and Gawain rode down into the dark dell.

He found the Green Chapel. It was no more than a mound and within it a cave – empty.

"Where are you then, Green Challenger? Stand forth." Gawain's voice echoed among the rocks.

"Wait there," came the dread command.

Gawain saw his giant foe, now on foot, leap over a stream, swinging the fearful axe like a twig. Now they stood face to face.

"You kept your word. Now take my blow."

Gawain bared his neck and bowed his head. Down swung the axe. But in the last moment he stole a swift glance upwards and flinched as he saw the razor-keen edge. "What?" roared his adversary. "I accepted your blow. Can you not take mine, or are you afraid?"

Once more Gawain, in shame, bowed his head. This time he stood like a rock. Down sped the axe, but now it halted just above his neck.

"What's this?" he shouted, "are *you* afraid, man? Strike." The giant raised the axe a third time. The razor edge flicked Gawain's skin. The blood shot out on to the snow. He sprang away, plucking out his sword. "Enough. No more blows without return."

The Green Man spoke calmly. "No, my friend. We are even. That little cut I gave you pays for the girdle that you accepted from my wife but did not tell me of. The other blows I did not strike home because you did not betray me, your host, with my wife."

Gawain, disgusted with himself, flung down the girdle. "I am ashamed that I was weak." His opponent handed back the sash. "No, keep it. You have redeemed your guilt. I asked my wife to tempt you and you would not yield."

"Who are you, Green Challenger?"

"My name is Bertilak. I came to Camelot to seek you out and put you to the trial."

"Why should you do so?"

"It was not by my will. But Morgaine, who rules me, bid me do it. Ride home, noble Gawain, for you have stood the test."

how lancelot won guinevere's kiss

When blossom lay like snow on the thorn, word came from the forest. The White Hart had been seen abroad. Camelot was mad with excitement, hounds bellowing as swift, rough-maned horses were saddled. Round Table heroes rushed to snatch the holly shaft spears and join in the hunt. This was the day when he who ran the White Hart down would be Guinevere's champion for the year and claim her kiss.

Kai and Bedwyr rode out side by side as always, sharing old memories. Gawain, green sash on arm to remind him of his weakness, which made folk love him more, sang as he trotted into the trees. Gareth, eager to outdistance his elder brother, was away with the dawn. Silent Mordred went his own way. Lancelot, his tunic like a flame, went last, as if it were no more than a game.

As the sound of horse and dog died in the distance,

Arthur and Guinevere had their awning set up on a green meadow hard by the woods and passed the day in talk and song. The chase was long – the White Hart made good sport, twisting and turning, luring the hounds into the mire, glimpsed in a flash through the green maze, only to vanish in the gloom.

But as the day began to die, the sacred beast was driven to the clearing, faltering with weariness. Shouts of the huntsmen were heard approaching. The White Hart broke cover to the cries of the handful of riders in hot pursuit.

Yet it was not the end. With mischievous speed the Hart swerved, Kai and Bedwyr's mounts crossed and fell in a heap. At the far side of the meadow Gawain appeared and the quarry stumbled his way as if to yield. But at the last moment, unseen out of the setting sun, came Lancelot. He sped so close to Gawain's spear that the point drew blood from his cheek. But the prize was his – the White Hart and the Champion's kiss.

Only Guinevere did not seem to see the red stain left on her face from his. Old Merlin said to me: "By the old gods' wisdom Arthur must hold the Spirit of the Realm against all challengers. He must beware."

"Whom should he fear?" I asked. "All here are loyal to the death."

Merlin answered: "Not treachery but love will be his undoing."

the story of ragnell's trick

Arthur grew restless with the passing time. In the idleness of his grandeur, the exploits of his warriors fed his discontent. Till one day in summer he put on his green hunting tunic, called for his horse and Cabal, his hound, and rode into the forest alone. A dozen rushed to mount and go with him but angrily he sent them back. "I'm not an old man. Leave me to hunt on my own."

"What if you meet danger?" shouted Kai.

"Then it's an old friend," called Arthur and spurred his horse.

All day he hunted, finding no game but enjoying the sweet air of the woods aglow with flowers. But when he turned, weary, to go home, the woods suddenly filled with mist. A white curtain was drawn around him. Lost, he climbed from his horse in a glade and sought to make out the way. And there he saw a tall figure.

"Sir," he called, "be good enough to show which way Camelot lies." To his dismay the figure turned, a huge man fully armed, sword drawn, his helmet shading his face. The voice was hateful. "If I had my way, Arthur, you would never reach home alive."

Arthur faced him. "Tell me your name and why you hate me. I will make amends. You see I am not armed for fighting as you are."

"My name is Gromer – no matter why I hate you. You have done evil in your time. Enough to die for."

"Then you're a coward if you will not give me chance to arm and fight you equally."

Gromer laughed harshly. "Armed or not, I could kill you. But I'll give you a year to live and meet me here. You must bring me the answer to one question – or you shall die."

"What question?"

"The question all men ask. 'What is it that women most desire?'"

At that, with a clap of thunder, the fearful figure vanished with the mist. Arthur went home to Camelot, deep in thought.

He kept his trouble to himself. But lightly asked the question of many people. He got as many different answers. What women most desire? Some said riches, some said flattery, some said kindness, some said bravery in men, some said vigour in bed. Each one was sure of their answer, yet the more answers he had, the more unsure was Arthur, and he went on with his search, right until the year was nearly over.

On the day before the one appointed he wandered brooding in the woods when he saw the strangest sight. A woman stood in his path, smiling at him, but horribly. Her body was ugly and gross, bulging here and there. More hideous still was her face with its foul nose and hanging lips.

"Good day, my lord Arthur," she said. Her voice gurgled, spittle flew from her lips. "You do not know me. I am Ragnell. I know you and I know what troubles you."

"How can you know?" Arthur turned to avoid looking at her, but she came closer.

"I know your life is forfeit tomorrow, and I know the answer that will save it."

"Then for God's sake tell me, lady," Arthur said.

"I will if you will grant a boon."

"What boon?"

"First grant it, then I'll tell."

With heavy heart Arthur said yes.

"My wish," said the ghastly crone with a leer, "is to marry the Prince of Men – Gawain."

Arthur was sick at heart. "I can only tell him what you ask."

"You tell him. He will do anything to save you. Meet me here at dawn tomorrow."

Laughing, the monstrous woman left him to his sorrow. And it was such that when Gawain met him soon after, right away he asked what troubled him. Arthur could not choose but tell his faithful warrior all.

"Have no fear," said Gawain, "if she were as ugly as sin itself, I'll do it for your sake."

Next day Arthur went out into the forest with first light. True to her word, Ragnell waited, with her gruesome smile.

"Greetings, Arthur. I know you kept your word. Now

I'll keep mine. What women most desire is power and dominion over men."

As she spoke, there was the clash of steel. Gromer, his face like thunder, stood before them. He cursed in fury. "Sister. You tricked me. I must release Arthur from his word. I would strike you dead in his place."

"If you could," answered Ragnell. "But you cannot. I am to be married to the greatest hero in the realm. Nothing can spoil my joy."

Taking Arthur's arm, leering at all they met on the way, Ragnell came home to Camelot in triumph. Not all the shrieks and tears from the ladies nor even Guinevere's pleas would move her. She would marry Gawain, right away, in public with the greatest pomp.

And it was done. Gawain, pale and manly, sat at his awful bride's side. It was more like a funeral than a wedding. Yet she grinned her ghastly grin. At last the sun set and they were alone in bed. Ragnell smirked at Gawain. "Well, husband, shall I have a kiss?"

"You shall have all a wife should have," he answered, taking her in his arms. And as he did, the foul hag vanished. He held the most lovely woman he had ever seen.

"Why, what are you?" he asked in awe.

"Your wedded wife, as you deserve, true Gawain," she replied. "Now you shall choose: would you have me ugly by day and fair by night? Or shall it be the other way? Say!"

For a second Gawain said nothing, then answered forthrightly: "You shall be as it pleases you, not me."

"Then it shall be as you please, my love," she said, and so it was. She was fair day *and* night. True love was theirs for five short years until Gawain's wife died and left him sad for ever after.

merlin's farewell

Hard by Camelot was a secret place where grew a bush, bright green and lush unlike any other round about. It was a spot sought out by men and women who wished to meet and let no one else know what they were doing.

One day, old Merlin came to Arthur with a grave face and asked him, "Is Guinevere true to you?"

"I know she is. What does this mean?" said Arthur angrily.

At that moment in she came to where they were. Merlin said nothing, but: "Lady, there is a green leaf in your hair, let me take it." He did so and left them.

"What troubles you, my Lord?" said Guinevere, touching her husband's hand gently. Sadly he told her what Merlin said and watched her face. Her grey eyes met his and she laughed.

"Merlin was wise, once. Now he is old and mad."

"Mad?"

"Allow me, my lord, to show you how his mind has strayed."

Next day Arthur and Merlin sat together. Guinevere came to them, leading a black-haired boy. "Tell me, Merlin. What is this lad's future?" she asked, but looked at Arthur as she spoke. Merlin looked down then said, "He will die soon, by hanging."

The boy ran out. But soon another youth with red hair was brought in. Guinevere asked Merlin the same question. "He will die pierced to the heart," he said and looked away.

Last came a girl with long yellow tresses. Merlin rose in anger, but said calmly, "And this one is fated to drown." The girl ran out and Guinevere turned to Arthur.

"Now I can tell you, my lord. These three children were one and the same, disguised. Now what do you say of Merlin?"

Arthur was silent. Merlin raised his hand. "Arthur, I have given you counsel for many years and always spoken truly. Now by a trick my word is cast in doubt. So I have no more to do here. We shall not meet again. I take my leave of you."

With that he turned and left Camelot for ever.

part five

the questing
spirit revived

in search of the
treasures again

With the years Arthur grew weary and out of spirits. An old wound in the thigh plagued him. Gloom fell on Camelot like a cloud. In the broad lands outside the ramparts all was not well. One bad harvest followed another. Folk complained. When times are hard the days of glory fade from memory. Warriors begged leave to depart to see to their own homes. Their people needed them and so they rode away.

Arthur watched them go and bitterly recalled his words to Kai: *When men no longer come here our name will be forgotten.*

One night those of the Round Table ate in silence. "There are only two means to revive our land," said Kai. "They are war and great adventure."

Arthur shook his great head: "War? We have had peace for many years. There are full-grown men who have never seen battle." He looked around him. "Who, in this realm or outside it, is strong enough to threaten war?" No one answered.

"Adventure?" said Kai. "Our exploits are history. They belong in song."

"Then sing, Taliesin," said Arthur to me. And I took up my harp.

I sang of ancient deeds, of Troy and Rome, of Bran, god-king, and his exploits beyond the sea. Inspired, unthinking, I sang on of how Bran's head was carried home and buried to protect the realm.

At the last moment I caught a warning in Gawain's eye, remembering how Arthur had dug up the Head of Bran. Quickly, hardly missing a note, I sang of the Treasures of the Island of the Mighty. The Horn of Bran, the jewelled Salver with endless food for all who need, the Cauldron of Eternal Life.

As my song ended, Arthur's fist thundered on the table. "The Treasures of the Island! If we had them now, all would be well. Peace and plenty for ever!"

Kai's voice rose bitterly: "They lie beneath the waves of Annwn. The Otherworld claims its own."

Arthur shook his head. "That is the strangest thing. The other night I saw the Treasures once more, in a dream. But now they were in a great palace, a lofty hall by a deep lake amid dark forests." He gazed around. "If I were young, I'd seek that palace out and win those Treasures back."

As ever, Arthur's words were like spurs. Next day, ten of his greatest warriors, Gawain and Lancelot at their head, rode out, north, east and west. All pledged to find and bring back the Treasures to Camelot, to restore their leader and his realm to their former power.

Yet here Fate twisted the cord. Or was some hidden hand at work? Those who sought failed in their quest. He who succeeded did not know what he found.

the story of peredur and the fisher king

Gawain and Lancelot rode north together, until one day in a forest glade a strange sight met their eyes: a young man, in peasant's tunic, running like a hound after two deer. The warriors shook their heads – the boy was simple.

Then they marvelled as he caught the deer and led them away. Gawain called after him. "What are you doing, boy?"

"Taking these goats back to my mother's herd, from where they escaped," he said.

"Those are not goats. They are deer," said Gawain.

"Deer?" The lad was puzzled. Then he looked at Gawain. "What are you, sir?"

"We are warriors from Arthur's war-band."

"What are warriors?"

Lancelot laughed. Who could be so simple? Gawain smiled, and answered the question – and others – about arms and armour, saddles, horses.

"What is your name, lad?" he asked.

"I am Peredur, son of Efrawg."

Gawain was amazed. How did the son of one of the North's great heroes know nothing of such things?

Now they came to a stockade, with thatched huts and horses. Peredur pointed to a stately lady in blue. "There is my mother."

Gawain and Lancelot dismounted and bowed low. The lady frowned on them. "I know who you are," she said, "and you are not welcome."

"Why, lady? What wrong have we done?" asked Lancelot.

"No wrong. Save this. I taught my son to know nothing of war and battle. When his father died, fighting, I hid him away. Now my Peredur has seen you he will want to be like you. Such is men's way. Thanks to you I have lost him."

With bowed heads Gawain and Lancelot went their way.

With sad heart Peredur's mother saw her son ride to the South in search of great Arthur. He sat on an old nag, its saddle fastened with rope. In his left hand he bore sharpened holly stakes to imitate the spears carried by heroes. His mother loaded him with food, with good advice and blessings. Her feelings were too hard to bear. She fainted and as Peredur looked back, he saw her in the arms of her servants.

But he thought only of adventure and rode on,

heedless of regret. As though he were still a child, he took food where he found it, kisses from girls or advice from strangers, all without hesitation. His innocence was round him like a cloak, his foolishness carried him on through peril and obstacle, his bravery was invincible.

But Death waited. One day a horseman in dark armour blocked his way. The horseman carried a golden cup. "See what I took from Arthur's table? None dared stop me," he boasted.

"That cup must be returned," said Peredur solemnly. The warrior laughed and, raising his spear, rode towards the lad. "Return it if you can," he sneered.

His spear-point aimed at Peredur's unguarded chest, the horseman drew ever closer. But in that instant Peredur let fly a holly stake which drove under the attacker's helmet, through his eye and laid him dead on the grass.

Peredur dismounted to strip him of his armour as though he were skinning a deer. But putting on the coat of chain mail was another matter. First he had it back to front, then upside down. Someone laughed. He looked up and saw a handsome, richly dressed man with two youths, one yellow- and one red-haired.

Seeing Peredur's angry look, the man spoke politely. "If it pleases you, we'll help you with your armour." This was done and then, as evening was drawing on, they took him to their home, a cheerful hall with blazing fire and loaded table.

After a meal the boys and Peredur played at quarter-staff. He beat them with ease.

"Are you skilled with swords?" his host asked.

"I never tried," said Peredur.

"Then take this blade," the man commanded, "and strike that pillar."

Peredur struck so hard, pillar and sword broke. "Place the two pieces together," he was told. The sword joined perfectly. "Strike again." This time sword and pillar broke and could not be joined.

"Two thirds of your strength have you gained," his host told him. "The rest you must gain by your own effort. One word of advice. Say little and see all."

The lord of the hall and his sons taught Peredur much in the skill of arms and sent him on his way. As before, innocence led him into danger, courage saw him through. Yet as time passed, he learnt to think before he spoke.

One day he came out of the dark forest. The track divided and at the parting of the way stood a tall tree. He marvelled, for one side of it was in full green leaf and the other blazed with fire. Only for a second did he hesitate, then took the path of fire. Before him opened an enchanted valley with broad lakes and rivers. On the water a grey-haired man was fishing from a boat.

Peredur hailed him, asking where he might find lodging for the night.

"In my home, stranger. Go to the valley head. You'll see it."

Peredur climbed to the valley head and was amazed to see amid the meadows a hall, magnificent as a palace. More amazing, he was expected: he was bathed and freshly clothed then led into a hall with lofty ceiling and heavily laden table. By a blazing fire a lord sat richly dressed.

"Welcome at last, but pardon me, sir, that I do not rise. An old wound troubles me."

"You expected me?" asked Peredur, surprised.

"I was the fisher in the boat," the lord said sadly. "I can no longer hunt. This is my only sport these days. Men call me the Fisher King."

But then he seemed to throw care aside: "Sit down with me and eat and drink."

Wondering at the King's words, Peredur sat. As the meal continued, so his wonder grew at the dishes placed before him, food and wine such as he had never tasted before, no earthly feast.

Then, when he thought the limits of his wonder had been reached, he saw an astounding thing. Youths and maidens passed in procession by the table. First a boy carrying a golden drinking horn, and then a maid a salver of the same hue, but studded with diamonds and pearls. The salver and the horn yielded up food and drink but never emptied.

As these strange and marvellous objects were borne before his eyes, the question burned in Peredur's eager mind: Whose was the golden horn, whose that fabulous dish? To know this answer was to know the very secret of life, he felt.

But as the question rose to his lips, a fearful wariness held him back. *Say little and see all*, the knight in the forest hall had told him. So, as the marvels passed by a second and a third time, he held his tongue. The moment passed.

At last he bade his host good night. For all his brooding, he fell asleep, till morning. He awoke to find the hall empty – no Fisher King, no knights, no servants.

Outside, his horse, unattended, cropped the grass. Bewildered, he rode from the enchanted hall. He felt as though the passing of a night had added years to him. He understood nothing of what he had seen, but he would never forget it.

Many days he journeyed till he came to a place ravaged by war. He found lodging in a fine hall, where he was received by the most beautiful maiden he had ever seen. Yet he was mystified, for the food served was poor, just bread and scraps of meat.

That night as he slept, the lady of the hall crept into his room and knelt by his bed. Her weeping woke Peredur.

"What troubles you, my lady?" he asked.

"Shame," she answered. "My brothers told me I must spend the night with you."

"But why?"

"Our stronghold is besieged by enemies who have

seized our lands. My brothers hope that you will fight for us in exchange for my love."

Peredur got up and took her hand. "Lady, you have my love and loyalty without question. Go to your bed and rest. Tomorrow I will fight your cause."

"You are a true hero," she replied.

At dawn next day Peredur armed himself and rode out on to the plain before the hall. One by one he challenged the besieging lords. One by one he threw them down and took their surrender, granting their lives if they restored the maiden's lands. She would have had him stay, but his mission was not ended till he had been accepted into Arthur's band. Bidding farewell, he rode on, but for all his journeying he did not forget this maiden, her face was always in his mind.

One winter day he stood on a hill in sight of Camelot's ramparts. A raven had killed its prey on the ground. The black of the wings, the white of the snow and the red of the blood recalled his love's hair, her face, her lips.

Deep in his daydream he was challenged roughly by Kai, who had ridden up to discover who he was. When Peredur did not answer, Kai set about to punish him but was knocked from his horse and staggered back, to the laughter of the onlookers.

Next came Gawain who, with a few polite well-chosen words, won Peredur's answer. So changed was Peredur that at first Gawain did not recognize the uncouth lad he had met in the North.

And so it was that innocent, foolish Peredur came to Arthur's Camelot in triumph as a hero.

return to the fisher king's hall

The great doors to Camelot's hall stood open, as Arthur and Guinevere and all their following gathered to honour Peredur as he took his place at the Round Table at last. In that joyful moment the sound of hooves was heard. Right into the crowded hall rode a woman mounted on a yellow mule. She was both richly dressed and fearfully ugly to look on and in her hand she bore a whip.

Pointing to Peredur, she demanded of Arthur, "Why are you honouring this youth?" Before Arthur could answer she spoke again. "He has told you of his great deeds. Has he told you of his shame?"

"What can this mean?" asked Guinevere. "What shame?"

"When he rode out in search of fame he left his mother dead of grief."

Peredur went white.

"I did not know."

"You did not seek to know. You did not turn. You did not think of her."

There was a terrible silence in the hall. But the lady had not done yet.

"What you did was wrong. What you did not do was worse."

"I do not know what you mean," cried Peredur.

"You saw wonders in the hall of the Fisher King. You saw the sacred jewelled Salver carried past, yet you did not ask its meaning: What is it? Who does it feed? Because of your silence, the wounds of the Fisher King are not healed." She looked round the hall. "Lands are laid waste. For want of heroes without fear to seek out truth and honour, the Treasures of the Realm are lost."

With that she turned her mule and rode away, leaving the hall in silence and bewilderment.

But her words struck home. Once more, the returned heroes of the Round Table set out on the Quest for the Treasures. Those who had doubted now believed that somewhere in that far enchanted palace they were to be found and by their magic the realm would be restored.

In vain the monk Cedwyn urged their lord to hold them back. "Who sent this woman?" he asked. "Where did she come from? She is not of this world and the treasures your heroes seek are heathen fantasies. While they ride off in vain pursuit of empty glory, your realm suffers."

But Cedwyn's words were lost in the clatter of hooves as Arthur's warriors rode out.

In the van galloped Peredur, eager to redeem his shame. And so he did, finding love and renown far from Arthur's Camelot.

Of Lancelot and Gawain, however, I have more to tell.

the story of lancelot's quest for the treasures

Lancelot rode out alone. He did not know where he was headed, for in truth his thoughts remained in Camelot with one he loved and should not love. Day after day he travelled till in the heart of the great forests of the West he lost his way. Confused and weary, he lay down beneath the trees, while his horse wandered, grazing the grass. Lancelot slept. And while he lay there, three women on horseback looked down on him. Morgaine and her sisters. They looked at one another and smiled. For here was the fairest man that woman ever saw. On that they were all agreed. What they could not agree on was whose love he should be. And so they carried him away, still sleeping, to decide the question at their leisure.

When Lancelot awoke he was in a strange, perfumed garden. A fountain splashed nearby. On a table close at hand were wine and fruit. One by one, three beautiful women came into the garden, smiled at him in welcome and went away.

Here was all a man could wish for. But as Lancelot found when he rose and looked around, there was no way out.

the story of gawain's quest for the treasures

To the north rode Gawain, heart free, with no questions on his mind, only memories of old loves, old battles. After many long days and many weary miles, he found himself towards evening on the shores of a dark lake amid high rocks. On an island across the water he saw a stronghold, whose ramparts glowed red-gold in the setting sun.

In its shadow he could see a boatman rowing towards him. Gawain hailed him: "Friend, will you row me yonder?"

"I can, but will not."

"Why?"

"Turn round. Here comes the Guardian of the Fort.

No one enters unless they overcome him. He is invincible. You are tired. Go back. You will find shelter."

Gawain saw a mounted warrior dressed in black like the night, thundering towards him, spear raised in menace. Hardly had Gawain turned his weary horse when the Guardian was upon him. He struck such a blow with his spear-point, the hero was flung to the ground. But at once he was on his feet and as his foe wheeled and charged again, Gawain snatched the warrior's spear-haft and wrenched him from the saddle.

In the dying light the rocks rang as their swords clashed. Exhausted as he was, Gawain still found the force to strike the blow which laid the Guardian of the Fort lifeless on the ground. Now he called upon the boatman.

"Row me over, friend."

And the boatman answered: "I will, but it will do you no good."

"Why so?"

"Who defeats the Guardian must take his place. Once in the stronghold you will never leave."

"Hold your peace, friend, and row," said Gawain, who was weary to death.

Once across the water he found the doors wide open. The hall inside was lit, a table laid with food. But no one came. He ate his fill then searched the stronghold, room by room; all echoed empty. He found a bedroom at last and a richly decked bed. Shedding his arms, he fell on the bed and slept like the dead.

Suddenly he awoke to a clap of thunder. The shutters flew open, great lights flashed, arrows and bolts plunged from the air and thudded round his head. The door flew open and a huge-maned lion roared upon him, mouth and fangs gaping.

Grasping his sword, Gawain rose and struck one mighty blow, severing the beast's head. In that moment all was silent. Darkness returned and Gawain slept again.

Once more he woke in full daylight. Around him there was noise and bustle. The place was full of folk. Servants entered, bringing him fine fresh clothes, then led him to the hall where many tables were laid. At each sat scores of women, young and old. As he entered, all rose and called out, "Hail to the hero who has set us free."

Three women, one white-haired and stately, one in middle life, one young and fair, came towards him, smiling.

"Do you not know us, Gawain?"

He was amazed and could not speak.

The first one said, "I am Ygerna, Arthur's mother, your grandmother. This is Gwyar, your mother and..."

"You are Ragnell, my wife," said Gawain to the third. "But I believed you had all gone from this earth."

All three women smiled. Then Gawain knew the meaning of the boatman's words: *Once in the stronghold you will never leave.*

my search for merlin

Now Camelot mourned as never in a time of peace. Lancelot had vanished. Rumours came that noble Gawain had died in a far-off country. Arthur and Guinevere grieved, each in their own way.

Arthur had another trouble weighing on him. For news came that a boy from the court had been found dead by strange means. The lad had climbed a tree by a brook with a rope to make a swing. He had lost his footing and as he fell, the rope had tightened round his neck. Plunging into the stream below, a stake in the water had pierced him to the heart. Thus, as Merlin had prophesied, the youth had died a threefold death, by hanging, piercing and drowning.

Arthur brooded over this matter and at last he called me to him and spoke low as if in secret. "Go, Little One, and seek Merlin. Sing to him through the wilderness, sing so softly that the words will reach his heart and not his ears. Go and bring him back."

I went at his command although I knew it was in vain. Four seasons lived and died as I wandered through the Island of the Mighty – mountain, moor, forest and marsh, but still I found no Merlin.

In the second year, I took ship to Little Britain, south across the sea and there in the misty depths of Brociliande Forest I found him. He sat by a small stone house, like a tomb amid the dark trees, his black robe in tatters, white hair like a shroud around him. At his feet a wild pig rooted for nuts. He talked to the pig gently of how he could not sleep, of a life of pain, wrongs done, enemies made, treachery between friends.

"Do not go, little pig. They cannot find us here."

But he knew I had come. He took my hand and talked as if he knew my errand.

"Seek not the Treasures, Little One. I have gathered them in, all save the Sword, which Arthur has. They are hidden like the old gods. Those who seek immortality will find it only in stories. Those who are remembered live for ever."

"Why are you hidden here, Lailoken?" I asked, using his old name.

He looked wildly at me. "The Lady of the Lake, she lured me here, imprisoned me. I loved, I was foolish. Now I can never leave."

Gazing round blindly, he said, "Nothing endures, not even great Arthur's victories. In the end the Saxons will conquer Logres and call it England. But the New Law will conquer them. Saints will rule, priests will rejoice and minstrels will starve." He took my arm and gripped it. "But listen, kings come, kings go. One day bridges will be built. There will be an end to war and the Island will be called by its old name of Britain again."

His head fell back, his eyes rolled. I went to the stream, brought water in my cap. Slowly he revived. We talked quietly of secret things, of how the world was made, where the wind blows from, who shaped the beasts and the birds and what was to be the fate of Arthur and Camelot. At last we embraced and said farewell.

He called after me. "Don't grieve for me, Taliesin. From my stone prison I can see the stars."

guinevere abducted

As I led my pony from the ship and took the road that runs to Camelot, the word reached me. A fresh blow had fallen on Arthur. In the season when the oak puts out fresh leaves, a young stranger had come to Camelot. He had lured Guinevere from the hall – it was whispered he pretended to carry news of Lancelot. But once in the forest he had shown his true colours. With armed men waiting in ambush, he had carried Arthur's lady away.

He was the Prince of the Summer Country, that Otherworld that lies west of Logres, the land where there are no storms nor lightning nor thunder, where no one dies and from where no one returns. He had chosen well the time to strike, for Arthur's warriors were scattered far and wide. Who knew where Lancelot was? Who knew if Gawain was alive?

Weary or not, I turned my pony and took to the roads again. Now I sang not softly as I had done for Merlin, but in full voice as if my life hung in the balance. Other bards and minstrels heard my song. They made it their own and sang it till there was no corner of the land that did not hear it.

It drew Mordred from the kingdoms of the North to Arthur's side. One by one the heroes came, saluted their chief then wheeled to gallop out once more, in tireless search for the Summer Country and the abducted Guinevere. Yet it seemed their seeking was in vain.

But song has powers to reach where no one goes. My tale was heard even in the depths of the rose-scented maze where Lancelot lay. It reached the heart of a young girl, herself a servant and a prisoner. She was in love with Lancelot. But hers was a love which understands the love of others. She saw his despair and, at great risk from Morgaine's anger, showed him the way from the labyrinth.

It sounded in the island fortress where Gawain lived among the women who loved him from the past. My song came to him like a dream. When he heard it, he begged Ygerna to release him from his bond and duty to be guardian of the stronghold. She shook her head sadly over him and said, "Do you know the fate that waits you in the world, son of Gwyar?"

He answered, "Even if I did, I must still go in search of Arthur's lady. I owe him my first loyalty. No other duty can outweigh this."

The boatman carried him over the dark water and back into this world again. He joined the band of heroes in search of the Summer Country. But it was not given to him or any other to succeed, but only to one guided by a love stronger than duty...

the story of guinevere's rescue

Lancelot rode by hill and plain, rough ways and smooth, till one day he met a strange sight – a dwarf driving a mule and cart. The carter hailed him.

"I know you, Lord. If you would find the one you seek, get down from your prancing horse and ride behind me."

Only for a fateful moment did Lancelot hold back, then mounted the cart. He rode through towns and villages, stared at and mocked. Folk said, "He must have done some vile thing, to ride like a man to the gallows."

"He looks like a hero," said some. But others answered, "Only a felon fit for hanging rides like that."

So, shamed and disgraced he came to the Summer

Country, where the carter set him down before the white ramparts from where its king and prince looked down. Lancelot looked up and called out, "Let he who holds Arthur's lady come down and face me."

At first the Prince looked on the challenge with contempt. But his father told him he could not choose but fight. So he went down, clad in mail white as the hawthorn, and fought with Lancelot.

He bore down Arthur's warrior, tired by his journey. But when it seemed Lancelot would fall, the women around Guinevere urged her to show herself on the walls of the ramparts. And at the sight of her, Lancelot's strength rose and he beat down the Prince of the Summer Country.

That night the King ruled that next day Guinevere should ride home with Lancelot. But love is impatient. After dark, Lancelot came to Guinevere's window. With desperate strength from long separation he broke the iron bars and that night they were together as never before in their lives.

Breaking the bars, the lover slashed his arms and blood poured out on to the bed. When it was found in the morning, the Prince in fury demanded that Guinevere should not be freed, unless her champion could defeat him a second time. Once more Lancelot and the Prince fought on the green below. Yet again Lancelot won the contest.

And still the Prince would not yield until his father

the King gave his judgement. Guinevere should return to Camelot for a year. If at the end of that time no hero could be found to defeat the Prince, she must go back to the Summer Country.

So Guinevere and her attendants set out for Camelot and there, at the end of a month, they were welcomed home.

The questing warriors one by one returned and once more there was feasting in Camelot as in the old days. For Guinevere, though, there was only sadness. Lancelot had not returned. He had vanished in the forests around the Summer Country. Led off the trail by false directions, he was imprisoned near a lonely lakeside tower by the Prince's servants.

A year passed and at the end of it the Prince of the Summer Country appeared before Arthur to make his challenge and, if it were not met, to take Arthur's lady back with him to the Land of No Return. Camelot's warriors were enraged at his demand. Only Arthur's promise of safe conduct saved the Prince from attack, even before the hour appointed.

With the dawn mists the white-mailed Prince appeared on prancing horse on the meadow before Arthur's hall. But who was to meet his challenge? Gawain appealed to Arthur and with his consent began to arm himself and mount his strong-backed horse. But even as they came face to face in the first rays of light, out of the morning sun came galloping a ragged rider, foul with mud and dust of long travel.

The crowd roared its amazement and delight as it recognized Lancelot. At once Gawain took off his coat of mail and helped his comrade buckle it on. For the third time Lancelot met the Prince of the Summer Country in single combat. And for the third and final time he brought him down and sent him from Camelot defeated. Guinevere was restored and every hero home. Not for many years had there been such rejoicing.

That night we listened as Lancelot told the tale of his escape. The Prince's sister, for shame at her brother's treachery, had found Lancelot's prison and set him free.

"For honour's sake – and perhaps a little for love," said Guinevere, and offered him the Champion's cup. All laughed and gave no thought to her meaning.

part six

the last battle

the song of
tristan and isolde

Three years passed, three golden years. Camelot days were like the days gone by, changing only with the season, with the hunt, the days of sport and mock battle, the nights of feasting, song and dancing.

At the heart was Arthur, our sun by day, our star by night. His hair was now pure white, his face softened from the fierceness which once struck terror into the very blood of foes. He was a father with his family around him, always there, and for that reason, forgotten now and then, he was content to gaze on our revels and dream of his youth.

Did he not see what was unfolding around him, under his eyes, or did he see and choose not to see the signs? There was love between two people dearer to him than any: Guinevere, the Spirit of the Realm, and Lancelot of the Lake, bravest and fairest of his war-band. The love was growing, and it was a love that had no room for him.

It was a love that had no tricks. Even their walking alone in the woods, their lingering in a hunting-lodge among the trees was done openly with nothing furtive. It was a love that thought itself invisible, and those

124

around who saw it – did not see.

Only one watched in the shadows. Silent Mordred waited for his moment. Now that Arthur grew old, Mordred came down from the North to spend more time at his uncle's side, saying things for his ears only.

It seemed to me that soon the secret would be out. Trouble and woe would follow. What could I do? Morgaine's words were always in my head. *"You shall know what other men do not, but you shall not make use of what you know."*

For days I pondered this until at last I saw a way, or thought, in my cunning, that I saw. One night as we feasted and Arthur turned to me, I took up my harp and sang, a story dear to all hearts.

I sang of Prince Tristan, the world's lover, sent to bring home Isolde, the young bride for his uncle, King Merch. How on the way to the marriage feast they drank, by chance, a potion and knew that they loved each other and could not bear to part. How their love, so lovely in itself, brought falsehood and treachery, death and destruction on all around them. How in the end, death came; they had loved and they had lost.

As I sang, I fixed my gaze, not on Arthur but on his Guinevere, and her Lancelot. I sang only to them, as a warning. But it was wasted. To lovers all is love.

But around the great circle of the Table someone was listening. Someone took heed. His dark eyes glowed like two star points.

mordred's ploτ

After the feast, in that dark hour that comes before dawn, I walked on the ramparts. It was full summer and the night air was sweet with the scent of flowers. All at once I heard two voices from the terrace below me. I listened with my singer's ear. Mordred spoke low and urgent.

"Lord, you cannot shut your eyes. They make a fool of you before your people. Their love is common fame."

Then Arthur's voice, low and rumbling like rolling rocks. "So they love each other? I am old but not blind. In my time I loved where I chose. What does it matter if they are true to one another and both true to me?"

I thought that Mordred had been silenced by this, but no – in a moment:

"Lord, you are wrong. They plan to betray you."

"What? Three times Lancelot threw his life on the scales to rescue her from the Summer Country."

"But why, why?" Mordred's voice grew more passionate. "To carry her off himself in his own time."

"No, no, you are wrong."

"I have it right. A short way from here in your hunting-lodge they keep horses saddled."

"To ride in the woods."

126

"And beyond – to a stronghold in the North, hard by Carluel. I tell you, Uncle, he will betray you; he wants your wife and your lands."

Arthur's voice was hard: "It is you who seek to rule, Mordred, not Lancelot."

"Not seek, Uncle, await. I have been promised. I can wait my time. He will not."

"Well, you are wrong and there's an end to it."

My blood ran cold as Mordred answered, "No, I am right and you are afraid to act."

In the stillness Arthur spoke again. "Do not call my courage into question, Mordred. No man does that and lives. Now, goodnight."

Next day I saw Mordred move about Camelot, going from one to another, pacing together with one, hand on another's shoulder, sometimes grave, sometimes smiling, always whispering. Unseen by him, I watched.

I saw one-armed Bedwyr laugh and walk away. Kai frowned and shrugged his broad shoulders. Gawain listened, grave and courteous, then shook his head. But Mordred was checked, not beaten, and I saw him go about again, this time with the younger warriors.

Walking in the gardens, I saw him sit upon a bench in close talk with Gareth Fairhands, Gawain's brother. His face eager – bright with innocence, eyes wide with amazement – he listened as grave Mordred talked. I saw them clasp hands and knew the fateful moment had come.

Throwing aside all caution, I went in search of

Lancelot, then of Guinevere. Neither could I find. What next?

At last when the sun was setting, I made up my mind. Quickly I saddled my pony and quietly I slipped away into the forest, silent on the mossy path. I meant to reach the trysting place and warn the lovers, but I had left it too late.

Even before I reached the glade around the lodge I heard the rasp and clash of steel blades in the twilight. Torches gleamed, men shouted, ran to and fro. One cried out in pain. There was a rush of galloping hooves. Two mounted figures almost rode me down and vanished through the trees into the gathering dark. The lovers had escaped.

But one lay on the ground, deaf to the noise around him, eyes dimmed, face pale, chest red with blood. Gareth Fairhands, struck down by Lancelot, was dying.

cedwyn's mission

Camelot was astir before dawn. Grim and gloomy, sad and angry faces gathered around the Table, white-haired Arthur at their centre. All looked at Gawain, his face lined with grief. Last night he had carried his young brother to the hall. His chequered tunic had another colour, stained with Gareth's blood. Slowly he spoke to Arthur, but his words were meant for all.

"There is a time for thought, for weighing rights and wrongs, before acting, for weighing friendship, comradeship, loyalty and duty. All of you know that I would rather win by fair words than by force of arms."

Kai nodded grimly. He knew his old comrade too well.

"But what can I do? My brother is dead. That blood, my blood, cancels out friendship. Lord, I must avenge my family for my brother's, my blameless brother's death." Gawain's voice broke. Men cleared their throats. Arthur gave a deep sigh and began to speak.

As he did, Cedwyn, who stood behind Arthur's chair, stepped forward, raising his hand. "Oh, Gawain, I grieve for this band of heroes wrenched apart by jealousy and hatred. The Red Dragon returns to its old ways and tears itself to pieces – no, let me say my say. Let no more blood be shed. Each drop that falls calls down another drop until the skies rain red, and God Himself is weeping."

He turned to Arthur and fell on his knees. "Let me go first to the North to Lancelot's stronghold. Let me beg Guinevere and Lancelot to return to Camelot in peace. Thus may a single quarrel not lead to open war."

Arthur looked at Gawain, who sat silent for a while, then said, "Blood cries aloud. But I will wait. Let Cedwyn do what he must. I do not seek war but justice, punishment for murder."

Gawain bowed his head. "I will wait for thirty days and nights then I shall ride with my sword drawn."

Cedwyn rode north on his little mule. One monk went before him carrying a white cross, another at his back with the picture of Our Lady. Ten days, twenty, five and twenty – we waited at Camelot and every day was like a year. Some brooded. Others prayed. Gawain, Kai and Bedwyr quietly sharpened swords, tested the hafts of spears, straps and shield buckles. No one sang, few spoke. Waiting was torment.

All but one day of Gawain's thirty had gone by when lookouts on the ramparts called. Out of the forests rode Cedwyn on his mule, behind him Guinevere on her horse, her face pale, her grey eyes closed.

Once more Cedwyn stood before the Round Table. "Chieftain, your wife is home. Half of my task is fulfilled with no blood shed."

"We thank you, Cedwyn," Arthur said.

"Rather, thank God," Cedwyn replied.

Gawain stood up from his place.

"But where is my brother's killer?"

"He would not return with me. But not from contempt or fear of you, Gawain. The truth is that he struck in self-defence, when men attacked him by night. He will not fight you, Gawain. He begs your forgiveness that, without meaning to, he caused your brother's death. Rather than stir up strife and bring fruitless war to the

Island of the Mighty, he and his following have taken ship and left our shores. He has chosen to lose his love for ever and live in exile. He has gone to his father's old stronghold in Little Britain, on the borders of Gaul. There in the depths of Brociliande he will make his peace with God."

to war, against lancelot

Cedwyn's words were heard and remembered but not heeded. The Old Law and the New contended and the Old Law triumphed. Life must match life and death cancel out death. Steel was honed, shields limed, horses saddled. The goddess of war washed battle shirts in streams that ran red.

With a great shout the Round Table spoke its will – the man who had betrayed Arthur and killed Gareth Fairhands must be brought to account. One, and one only, spoke against and that was Kai, Arthur's old battle companion. "Do not leave the Island," he urged Arthur. "Let others lead the war-band. Stay here and guard your own."

Arthur shook his great white head. "If I am wronged,

131

another cannot put it right." He spoke low to Kai. "Take picked men. Escort Guinevere to Kelliwic. Guard her with your life." Kai laid his hand on Arthur and turned away.

Then Arthur turned to Llachau, his quiet son, who stood beside his chair. His eye had a tear in it. "Llachau. I have been hard on you. You did not deserve it. Will you sail with me on this last expedition?"

Llachau said, "There is nothing to forgive, Father. But I will not go with you. I will stay with Kai. Farewell." They embraced and Arthur's son followed the old warrior from the hall.

Our war-band sailed, the ship's prow turned towards the south. There was no song, no shout, no sound but the wind. With the night the breeze dropped, the sails hung limp and the flotilla drifted. Arthur slept, his men around him, but as the wind freshened with the dawn, he woke and seized my arm.

"Ah, Little One, you're there. I dreamt a dream that our great hall was falling, axe strokes like a giant's felled its timbers."

I whispered. "An omen? Will you turn back?"

But he answered, "No, we are nearer to tomorrow than yesterday. We must go on and meet our fate."

how arthur failed to see the true peril

We landed on the shores of Little Britain, marched and rode until we came by the frontier with Gaul. There on a hill above the forests, we reached Lancelot's stronghold, with its great ramparts, ditch and palisade. His band was small in number, we were many more. One fierce assault like the wave of the sea and it would go down.

But Gawain told Arthur, "Let two lives go in the balance and no more. Call Lancelot down and I will fight him in your cause and mine."

It was so. They who had fought side by side so many times now turned spear and sword blade on each other.

All that weary day, Gawain and Lancelot fought. None was more skilled than Gawain, none stronger than Lancelot. And as the noon hour passed, Gawain grew weaker. They fought like men in a dream, the blood seeping through their coats of mail. As the sun went down, one heavy blow to Gawain's head brought a halt to the combat. He was carried to Arthur's tent. "Tomorrow," he told his chieftain, "we shall fight again to the end."

But it was not to be. That night a messenger on a

sweat-soaked horse brought dire news to Arthur. Mordred had risen against him with an army – Picts, Saxons, Britons who bore grudges. Swooping on Kelliwic, he had snatched Guinevere, abducted her to the North. Defending Arthur's lady, Kai and Llachau had fought to the death.

That was not the end of Arthur's woe.

Heavy-hearted, we lifted the siege of Lancelot's stronghold and rode north to our ships again. In all our hearts the thought lay heavy. We had chosen the wrong battle and the wrong foe. We had turned our back on the true peril.

None felt this more than Gawain, lying wounded in the prow as the cliffs of Logres gleamed in the morning light. The understanding gave him strength. He whom we had thought wounded to death got to his feet, buckled on his sword and chose three yellow-hafted spears for his left hand.

As our keels grated on the shore, we saw the dunes dark with a defending force, with Mordred's banner flying over them. They meant to stop us landing. With Arthur held in his ships, Mordred would be master. Who could rally against him if the Boar of Cornwall could not raise his standard?

Gawain put on his helmet and saluted Arthur. "My thirst for revenge led you out of Britain. Let me repay my debt and lead you back again."

Arthur would have held him back. "Your wound is too

deep," he told Gawain. But Gawain only laughed. "Then I'll not feel it when they strike again."

With these last words he swung down from the ship, splashed in the waves and stamped on to the sand. And Arthur's war-band followed as one man. Spear beat on shield, blade hacked mail, the assault was savage but soon over. Clearing the shore, we drove Mordred's men before us.

mourning at camelot

Before a second day had passed, Arthur had raised his standard near Camelot, rallying his forces from far and wide. He pitched his war-tent on the plain where the Cam runs towards the sea.

That day Kai and Llachau were brought home from Kelliwic, where they had fallen. Gawain too, who died as he cleared the beach for Arthur's coming back to Britain. On the eve of the battle, as Arthur's warriors gathered round him, I sang:

> *"I saw Llachau, true to his trust*
> *Quiet in the hall where boasts were made*
> *Fierce in battle, when blue blades ran red.*

Kai, taunting his foes with his tongue
As he laid them low
His rage was a banner;
Kind to the best,
Without mercy to the worst."

Last of all I sang of Gawain while all wept:

"No woman bore so fair a hero
Beloved of women.
Courteous in sharing
Gracious in manner
Fearless in fighting
Ordering the spear hedge.
Green grass grows over him
None can take his place."

Night died, the dawn was grey on the hills to the east when Cedwyn came to Arthur.

"Give me leave, lord, to go a last time to Mordred. Your two armies have gathered all the finest in the realm. Nothing but evil can arise if you fight one another. Let me try once more to reconcile you with your nephew."

The warriors standing near bristled like boars at these words.

But Arthur looked at the monk with kind eyes and said sadly, "I have lost everything, wife, sons, comrades.

Where can I go on the face of the earth?

"I have closed my eyes to wrong. I have done rash deeds. Now I must account for all my life. I must fight one last fight."

the battle of camlann

How can I sing of Camlann, worst and most futile of conflicts, where as foretold the Red Dragon tore itself to pieces and the fellowship of the Round Table, bravest of warriors, went down? I would wash it from my mind but I am fated to recall.

All day was uproar and confusion, a thunder like the sea on rocks. Swift horses, white shields red-stained, screams of the fallen, ranks broken, no side gaining. Wounded and weary, the hosts might have made a truce. But lies were told, false messages passed, and so the fight went on.

As the day ended, Arthur, like a stricken bull, shook his head to clear his eyes of the blood streaming down and took Caliburn between his two hands. Calling his men around him like a wedge, he drove into the mass of Mordred's men, splitting them apart.

Face to face with his nephew, white hair flying

beneath his helmet, Arthur fought his last single combat, struck his last blow and received his last wound. Both fell to earth, the sun went down. Camlann was over.

farewell to arthur

Seven of us came alive out of that battle. I led them to the dark shore where we laid our hero down. I knew what must be done and what would come to pass.

I knew that Morgaine and her sisters would come in their swan-necked boat. Arthur would go with them to Avalon, the isle of sunshine and apples, to be healed of his wounds for our land's sake.

He gave Caliburn to one-armed Bedwyr, instructing him to throw it into the lake. So, unwillingly, the old warrior took it to the shore, but could not bear to throw it in. Twice Arthur sent him back, gently but sternly, till white arms from the water took the Sword back to the Otherworld from where it came. The last of the Treasures of the Island of the Mighty had gone to its crystal home.

So Morgaine took her Arthur to the West and me, his minstrel, she sent away again, saying, "Go, Taliesin. Sing your Song of Arthur."

epilogue

I shall praise you, Boar of Cornwall, Chief Dragon,
War Leader of Britain, who gave his land
a generation's peace.
I praise you, enricher of your country, giver of gifts —
amber and gold, torques and spurs, horses from your herd —
generous as the rolling wave.
I see you again in Camelot, hall without fault,
where equal heroes sat at the Round Table without dissent
or envy.
I see you on the white-fleeced couch, passing the mead
horn, calling for a song, till the night paled into day.
I see you like a rock in battle, never shaken,
none more steadfast.
I shall sing of you while I have voice in my throat,
our Boar, our Raven.
I see you riding in the Wild Hunt above the trees,
brightest of stars in the Northern Heaven.
When Morgaine has healed you, you will return in a
swift ship, scatter our enemies and restore us to our peace.
You will live, O Arthur, as long as people know
your story.
I shall not die as long as I can sing.

WHY I WROTE THIS BOOK

The story of Arthur, doomed hero, who will yet return to save his people, still holds us after 1,500 years. Who was he? Where was Camelot? Is it history, is it legend?

Other questions have intrigued me since I first read this story in Sir Thomas Malory's famous fifteenth-century version. If Arthur was "King of the English", why did he fight to drive out the first English invaders? If the "pure" knight, Galahad, was greater than Kai, Gawain or Lancelot, why did I find him sanctimonious in contrast to them? More baffling, if Morgaine was an evil murderess, why did Arthur find healing in her arms on the Isle of Avalon?

These questions and others are my reasons for this retelling. All are contradictions introduced by Malory's version, and their answers lie in the history of the legend.

Arthur's legend began in the fifth century AD, after Britain's Celtic people failed to keep out the invading Saxons. But someone, a mighty war leader, had, it seems, delayed the Saxon victory, giving the British a generation's peace. Around his name gathered tales of gods and heroes from the deeper, Celtic past.

These tales were kept alive in the bardic tradition of old Wales and Cornwall. Like Arthur, they would not die. A millennium later, princes were still named after

Arthur. The legends grew and spread, through Brittany to Normandy and France to Germany, Italy, Scandinavia. Although they were full of pagan magic, monks in their cloisters loved them more than the lives of saints, French troubadours sang them, Cornish villagers came to blows with those who claimed Arthur was dead.

In the thirteenth century, when Christianity needed to harness knightly martial prowess for the Crusades, the Arthur legend was adapted, refined, converted to new spiritual meaning. The old pagan Treasures – the cauldron of everlasting life, the horn of plenty – became changed to the Grail of Christian faith. Old heroes such as Kai (deemed too "heathen") or Lancelot (deemed too sinful) were superseded by a new one, Galahad. In his aura, the others became less and worse. Morgaine, the pagan goddess figure, who incited men to great deeds, was turned into a temptress luring them to destruction.

Sir Thomas Malory, translating these tales from the French, made them a fable for *his* time, the late fifteenth century. Arthur became "King of England", when in fact at that time there was no single king.

Yet the older legends lived on and it seemed to me worthwhile to reconstruct them. By going back beyond Malory, to the time when Arthur may have lived, when Celtic Britain yielded to Saxon England, when pagan belief was beginning to be absorbed into Christianity, I felt I might find a fuller measure of the tragedy of Arthur which was the tragedy of his people and their way of life.

So, in my retelling there is no Galahad, indeed there are no Sir Knights at all. Instead there are warriors – and they don't live in fifteenth-century turreted castles, but fifth-century strongholds. The Otherworld is not in Heaven, but all around the living.

To weave together stories, poems and fragments into a coherent "Song of Arthur", I borrowed the voice of Taliesin, the legendary bard. To find this voice, I have drawn on editors and translators to whose achievements I am deeply indebted. The most important of their works are listed opposite.

R.L.

BIBLIOGRAPHY

Ashe, Geoffrey
  Arthurian Britain,
  Longman, 1980

Bromwich, Rachel (ed.)
  *Triads of the Island of
  Britain*, University
  of Wales, 1979

Bromwich, Rachel &
Jarman, A.O.H. (eds.)
  The Arthur of the Welsh,
  University of
  Wales, 1991

Graves, Robert
  The White Goddess,
  Faber, 1961

Griffin, T.D.
  *Names from the Dawn
  of British Legend*,
  Llanerch, 1994

Guest, Lady Charlotte,
  (trans.)
  The Mabinogion,
  London, 1906

Hall, L.B.
  *The Knightly Tales of Sir
  Gawain*, Chicago,
  1976

Henken, Elissa R.
  *Traditions of the Welsh
  Saints*, D.S. Brewer,
  Cambridge, 1987

Jackson, K.H. (ed.)
  O Gododdin,
  University of
  Wales, 1969

Jarman, A.O.H.
  *The Legend
  of Merlin*,
  University of
  Wales, 1976

Jones, Gwyn &
Jones, Thomas
  (ed./trans.)
  The Mabinogion,
  Dent, 1993

Kibler, William W.
  (ed./trans.)
  *Chretien de Troye's
  Arthurian Romances*,
  Penguin, 1991

Mason, Eugene
  (trans.)
  Arthurian Chronicles,
  University of
  Toronto, 1996

Stewart, R.J. (ed.) &
Matthews, John
  (trans.)
  *Merlin through
  the Ages*,
  Blandford, 1995

Skene, W.F.
  *The Four Ancient
  Books of Wales*,
  Edinburgh, 1868

Thorpe, Lewis
  (ed./trans.)
  *Geoffrey of Monmouth:
  The History of the
  Kings of Britain*,
  Penguin, 1966

First published 2000 by Walker Books Ltd
87 Vauxhall Walk, London SE11 5HJ

This edition published 2001

2 4 6 8 10 9 7 5 3

This book has been typeset in Weiss and Francesca

Printed and bound in Great Britain by
The Guernsey Press Co. Ltd

British Library Cataloguing in Publication Data:
a catalogue record for this book is
available from the British Library

ISBN 0-7445-7874-4